League, Love

by M. Gorman

Copyright © 2025 by M. Gorman

All rights reserved. No part of this book may be reproduced, stored in a retrieval system, or transmitted in any form or by any means—electronic, mechanical, photocopying, recording, or otherwise—without the prior written permission of the publisher.

This is a work of fiction. Names, characters, places, and incidents are either the product of the author's imagination or are used fictitiously. Any resemblance to actual events, locales, or persons, living or dead, is entirely coincidental.

Printed in the United States of America.

Author's Note

The Junior League has been many things over its more than 100-year history: A launchpad for community leaders, a steward of social change, and a place where women have come together to shape the cities and causes that they love. Founded in 1901 by Mary Harriman, the League has grown into one of the most impactful women's volunteer organizations in the world — driven by the belief that women can truly make a difference.

For me, the League has been more than a line on a résumé or a set of committee assignments. It has been a home. A proving ground. A place where I've met some of the most thoughtful, driven, and generous women whom I've ever known. Through late-night event prep, public advocacy, and the kind of quiet, unglamorous work that rarely gets noticed, I've learned what it means to lead with both strength and softness — and to show up, again and again, even when no one's watching.

This novel is a love letter — to tradition, to friendship, to belonging. It's a tribute to the ways women build, lift, and carry one another, often without recognition. And it's a celebration of what it means to find your voice — sometimes in high heels, sometimes in sneakers, but always, always together.

Thank you for reading.

With gratitude,
Mary Kate Gorman

Chapter 1: September – Homecoming

The Astor House radiated a kind of quiet grandeur, its checkered marble floors gleaming beneath the soft glow of crystal chandeliers, shadows dancing off the rich mahogany wainscoting and decades old oil portraiture.

The air carried a faint scent of beeswax polish, mingling with the sharper bite of the last of summer's freshly clipped hydrangeas arranged in towering chinoiserie. The room buzzed with the sound of voices—each conversation wrapped in layers of sophistication. Members of New York's Junior League were busy catching up after the summer holiday, sipping champagne in the storied mansion on Manhattan's upper east side.

Charlotte Hastings stood at the threshold, her gaze sweeping the room as she tried to settle her nerves. It was her first official Junior League event, and while she'd been preparing for months, she couldn't shake the feeling of stepping into another world. A world where the stakes were high and the expectations even higher.

New York had always been a place of possibility, but here, possibility felt like something more—a legacy, a story that had been written long before she arrived. It was a tradition of giving back, of creating influence, but also a place where connections were everything. Charlotte exhaled slowly, centering herself. This house had seen hundreds, maybe thousands, of women pass through its rooms. Some would move on, some would stay. She wanted—no, she needed—to be one of the ones who stayed.

As Charlotte moved through the house, ascending the regal sprawling staircase that beckoned all visitors from the foyer, the walls around her seemed to pulse with history: framed oil portraits of storied League founders watched over the evening's festivities, their expressions both approving and impossible to read. Somewhere in the distance, the muffled pop of a champagne cork punctuated the low hum of conversation.

The Junior League had been a natural next step for her after graduating from the University of Virginia. A way to find her place, to get involved, to meet people outside of her demanding work as an apprentice art appraiser at Sotheby's. The League would be a test, not just of her ability to connect or contribute, but of how she could learn to navigate the balance between contributing to a larger cause and remaining true to herself.

    She adjusted the hem of her dress – a simple, navy piece that offset her shiny auburn hair – that she had chosen specifically for this occasion. Elegant, but not flashy. Warm enough to ward off the crisp September evening. Charlotte didn't want to stand out for the wrong reasons, but she also didn't want to fade into the background. Fashion in New York was always a delicate balance – It was never cool to look like you were trying too hard (every girl fancied herself a modern-day Carolyn Bessette) but you still had to have the "right" look – If you know you know.

    "Charlotte!" A voice called, familiar and warm. A small shiver went down her spine.

    Charlotte turned to see Avery Sinclair, her former Chi Omega sorority sister, walking towards her with the same confident stride she remembered so well. Back then, Charlotte had always admired Avery from a distance—her self-assuredness, her natural social grace, her ability to effortlessly move through any crowd.

Avery had always been one of those people who seemed to glide through life effortlessly, as a senior during Charlotte's freshman year, her style influence alone spawned a thousand campus group chats, and now, standing in front of Charlotte, it was clear that nothing had changed. Her dress—a deep emerald green Elie Saab—flattered her figure, tanned cinnamon skin and brilliant blonde hair in a way that seemed almost too perfect. It was the kind of thing that would catch your eye but never scream for attention.

Avery smiled as she reached Charlotte, her eyes lighting up with recognition. "I didn't expect you to be here tonight! It's a relief, actually. You always were good at handling these kinds of things."

Charlotte chuckled, feeling her nerves start to ease just a little. "Well, I'm trying. It's all a little overwhelming, though, isn't it?"

Avery's gaze flicked over the room, taking in the lavish surroundings with a quick, practiced glance. "It's a lot to take in at first, but you'll get used to it. And don't worry, there's no rush. You'll find your rhythm. Just make sure to play your cards right. *People will be watching.*"

Charlotte couldn't help but smile at Avery's candidness – and shirk at her veiled threat. There was a slight edge to her words, a hint of competition that Charlotte hadn't missed. Avery had always been sharp, but here, in this environment, the stakes were higher. Charlotte knew that this year would be a test—not just of her ability to fit in, but of how she could contribute and carve out her own space.

"Well, I'll try not to embarrass myself too much," Charlotte said, her smile easing the tension between them.

Avery laughed, but there was an unmistakable spark in her eyes, a bit of rivalry that seemed to hover between them. ""You'll be fine. Just remember, it's all about relationships. That's what this whole thing is about—getting to know people, making connections, contributing where you can. We'll help each other out, okay? But just so you know," Avery added, her voice lowering slightly, "I'm on the House Committee this year. It's where all the action happens."

Charlotte raised an eyebrow, intrigued. "House Committee?"

Avery nodded, her lips curving into a small, knowing smile. "It's the committee that handles the Astor House—our history, our legacy. We plan the events here, manage the space, all of that. Trust me, there's nothing more prestigious than working in this building – and this committee is *very particular* about who gets to join."

Charlotte felt a flutter in her chest. The Astor House was more than just a venue; it was a symbol. The historic building had hosted countless galas, fundraisers, and social events since the Junior League had established its headquarters there decades ago. The history of the League and the city itself was woven into every inch of the space, from the original murals on the walls to the antique furniture that lined the halls. It was a legacy of New York's elite, and for someone like Charlotte, it was a privilege to be here—even if she was only a provisional member.

Avery, noticing the direction of Charlotte's thoughts, smirked. "You'd be surprised how much influence you can have just by being in the right room. But don't worry," she added with a wink, "I'll make sure you're not lost in the shuffle."

Charlotte nodded. She had always been a little intimidated by Avery back in college, and, with good reason.

Before they could chat any longer, a voice rang out over the crowd.

"Ladies, if I could have your attention, please."

Everyone quieted as an elegant, grey woman stepped forward. Her hair was coifed neatly and her tailored but well-worn tweed suit exuded the kind of quiet, WASPY authority that was inherited, learned – you couldn't buy this off the rack. This was Barbara Fairchild, a Sustainer of the League and a respected member whose wisdom and insights had shaped the organization for decades.

Charlotte could feel the shift in the room as Barbara addressed the group, her tone calm but commanding.

"In many ways," Barbara began, her voice carrying a quiet strength, "New York is a small town. We think of it as a vast city, but in truth, it's a place where connections matter more than anything. Whether you're in the art world or the nonprofit sector, you'll find that the people you meet here will become a part of your story, for better or for worse. The same is true for this organization."

Barbara's gaze swept over the room, her presence commanding but not overbearing. The crowd nervously gripped the stems of their dainty wine glasses, manicures and heirloom diamonds gleaming.

"The Junior League is a small community," she continued. "And like any community, the relationships we build here have the power to shape our lives. We come together to make a difference, to support each other, and, yes, to grow. But remember, in a small community like ours, your actions will speak louder than anything else. The way you carry yourself, the work you put in, the way you show up – that will define who you are here."

Charlotte felt her pulse quicken as the weight of Barbara's words settled in. This wasn't just about parties and events. This was about building trust, contributing meaningfully, and being part of something bigger than herself. She could feel the quiet challenge in Barbara's voice – this would be a test of her own character.

Barbara gave a small, knowing smile before continuing, her voice softening just a touch.

"That said, remember this: You are not alone. In this League, you are part of a team. We are here to support each other, to lift each other up, and to make this city – and the world – a better place. So, let's begin. Please refer to the instructions on the sheet in front of you to find your committee pairing and how you'll be spending the rest of your year."

The buzz of conversation slowly returned to the room, but Charlotte's thoughts were still with Barbara's words. A small community. A place of trust. A place to contribute. As she scanned the sheet that had been handed to her when she walked in, her mind raced.

Charlotte's fingers tightened around the elegant, bone colored paper as she scanned the list. Emerald was the official house color and all provisional names were printed in sprawling script – Annabel, Ashely, Blake, Bunny, Cassandra and then… Charlotte.

She wasn't sure what she was expecting, but she was certain that whatever committee she was assigned to would set the tone for her entire year. There she saw her name, in sprawling script, Charlotte Hastings, assigned to the House Committee, under the direction of Ms. Avery Sinclair.

There was a soft murmur of agreement among the women in the room as committees and provisionals began to slowly assemble in pockets, and Charlotte caught Avery's eyes across the crowd, a smirk playing at the corner of her mouth – An unspoken acknowledgment passing between them. *Welcome to the game.* Charlotte wasn't just here to join a club. She was here to prove herself.

Charlotte straightened her shoulders and moved across the room to join her committee, the soft click of her block heels muffled by the thick, Persian rug that stretched like a river of burgundy and navy down the center of the hall.

The year was just beginning. And she was ready.

***

The next morning, Charlotte's alarm blared far too early, the opening synths of ABBA's sparkly disco anthem "Gimme! Gimme! Gimme! (A Man After Midnight)" shrieking through the room.

It was, objectively, the worst song to wake up to – obnoxious and high-pitched – but she couldn't bring herself to change it. Too many late nights dancing barefoot at beachside bars on Nantucket, too many memories of Ivy spinning her around under strings of fairy lights, salty air clinging to their skin.

Still, this morning, it made her want to throw her pillow across the room.

With a groan, she rolled out of bed, duvet slipping to the floor, tangling around the crisp white sheets beneath it. All of Charlotte's bedding was white – partly because it looked clean and classic, but mostly because it was easier to bleach out the inevitable stains from the late-night takeout, she swore she'd stop ordering.

Charlotte couldn't cook to save her life – eggs were ambitious, pasta a gamble – so she lived in a state of uneasy truce with New York's endless parade of delivery menus.

She was already late.

Their apartment – a small, sun-dappled two-bedroom in the heart of Lenox Hill – was a classic prewar, all crown molding and creaky floors. There had been one or two cockroaches when she first moved in, but they were already dead, so it hardly counted. Above one of the Upper East Sides most famous boulangeries, every morning smelled like bread and butter.

Charlotte's roommate, Ivy Ashford, had inherited the rent-controlled gem from her grandmother, who had once been the toast of Park Avenue in the 1960s. Now, it was filled with a mismatched but charming array of vintage finds: mid-century chairs upholstered in worn velvet, stacks of old Town & Country magazines, and Ivy's rescue doodle, Clementine, who was currently sprawled across the Persian rug, enjoying a breakfast of freshly poached, wild-caught salmon tail thumping lazily.

"You're late," Ivy called from the kitchen, her voice amused but not surprised.

Charlotte yanked on a cream silk blouse and slid into a camel wool skirt, pulling on low block heels as she moved. "I know!" she shouted back. "Barbara Fairchild's voice haunted my dreams."

Ivy poked her head around the doorframe, barefoot and wrapped in a vintage Pucci robe, a mug in hand.

She was, without question, the most gorgeous person Charlotte had ever known – an effortless kind of beauty that less confident women could never quite accept as a friend. Maybe Charlotte couldn't either, if they hadn't known each other since before they were babies. Ivy's long, dark hair, deep and glossy, had never been dyed. Her gorgeous deep skin, untouched by anything more aggressive than a swipe of rosehip oil, seemed to glow even in bad lighting. She had that rare, arresting magnetism that couldn't be bottled or bought – it just was.

They had grown up together spending summers on Nantucket, a small island off the coast of Massachusetts. Best friends whose moms had been best friends, their summers a blur of saltwater, sand, and the smell of sunscreen. Bike rides to the beach, bonfires that stretched into star-streaked nights, hours spent elbow-to-elbow reading on porches cooled by sea breezes. In a city of curated alliances, Ivy was—without question—home.

Charlotte smiled at the sight of her, feeling a small knot of tension ease in her chest.

"That's what you get for signing up for the Ladies Who Guilt Club," Ivy said breezily, disappearing back into the kitchen.

Charlotte laughed, grabbing her tote and phone. "You know why I joined."

Ivy's voice floated out. "Because your mom would've wanted you to."

Charlotte paused, her fingers brushing the thin gold chain she wore – a simple piece her mother had left her. Her mother, who had spent weekends volunteering at literacy clinics and hosting Junior League fundraisers. Her mother, who had worn pearls with everything, even jeans.

"She was right," Charlotte said softly. "It's about more than just the champagne."

Ivy reappeared, Clementine's leash in one hand, a vegan, homemade croissant tucked into the crook of her arm. "Maybe. But I'll stick to rescuing fur babies and avoiding committees, thanks."

Minutes later, they were bundled up and walking briskly toward Sotheby's, Clementine trotting along proudly in a tiny Barbour jacket. The September air was crisp and dry, the kind of morning that hinted at sweaters and cider just around the corner.

They made their usual stop at Sant Ambroeus on Madison, slipping into line behind a collection of impossibly polished New Yorkers – immaculate jeans, structured bags, oversized sunglasses shielding faces too perfect to be real. Ivy ordered a soy cappuccino; Charlotte stayed true to form with oat milk latte and an almond biscotti.

As they waited, Ivy nudged Charlotte playfully with her shoulder. "You really need to change that alarm."

Charlotte grinned, cradling her coffee. "You're just too cool to appreciate ABBA."

"I'm not too cool," Ivy said, mock-offended. "I just have taste."

"Same thing." Charlotte laughed. "Besides, it's basically our Nantucket anthem."

Ivy rolled her eyes but smiled anyway. "Only after three Aperol spritzes and someone playing it on a speaker that's about to die."

Charlotte laughed again, remembering hazy, perfect summer nights driving cars on the beach with music blasting, the sky wide open and full of stars. The world full of possibilities.

They crossed Madison Avenue together, the sun striking gold off the windows above them, heading toward the soaring glass entrance of Sotheby's.

"So," Ivy said, shifting topics as she dodged a delivery bike, "are you ready for the chaos today?"

Charlotte groaned dramatically. "Barely. And we still have to deal with Harrison."

Ivy made a noise somewhere between a laugh and a groan. "Oh, Mr. Preservation Society himself. How could I forget?"

So far, all their interactions had been through terse, punctilious emails, peppered with obscure architectural references Charlotte had to quietly Google on the side.

She hadn't met him in person yet, just pieced together an impression from old BFA gala photos and glossy charity event coverage. Tall. Broad-shouldered in tailored Tom Ford. The kind of aristocratic good looks that managed to look both old-world and impossibly current. He was exacting about provenance, relentless about detail, and entirely too good-looking for Charlotte's peace of mind – All brooding good looks, tall in the way old houses were tall, with a kind of deliberate, measured grace.

"Tall, broody, bossy," Ivy said, ticking adjectives off on her fingers. "Basically your type."

Charlotte rolled her eyes but didn't argue.

"Impossible and hot," Ivy amended, smirking. "Accuracy is important."

"Intelligent, well-read, wordly," Charlotte countered.

They pushed through the revolving doors into the soaring marble lobby, the hum of Sotheby's starting to pulse around them.

Charlotte tucked a strand of hair behind her ear, feeling her nerves – and excitement – tighten in her chest.

Jamie Harrison was standing over her desk and he was taller - much taller - in person and she was wholly unprepared.

***

He wore a charcoal gray jacket, sleeves pushed up slightly at the cuffs, revealing strong, sinewy forearms and an expensive watch that somehow managed to look lived-in rather than flashy. His dark hair was a little messier than her well-wrought research would have suggested, and his face – sharp jaw, straight nose, dark blue eyes – was less polished, more rugged up close.

In short, he looked exactly like the kind of man who could restore a crumbling mansion with his bare hands and still make a black-tie event by sunset. There was a certain gravity about him, an air of command that seemed less about vanity and more about habit – like he was used to people listening when he spoke, even if he didn't say much.

Charlotte sat down so quickly her chair almost tipped backwards, spilling a splash for her pricey oat milk latte on the expensive leather blotter than guarded the antique wood of her desk.

"Mr. Harrison," she managed, hoping her voice didn't crack. It definitely did.

For a moment, he simply looked at her, as if cataloging everything in front of him. Not coldly, but intently—almost too intently.

He smiled—a slow, real smile that started at the corner of his mouth and seemed to take its time getting to his eyes.

Then he inclined his head slightly, a gesture so formal it might have been from another century.

"No need for 'Mr.,'" he said, voice low and even. "Just Jamie."

Jamie.

"Right. Of course. No problem. Just Jamie." Flustered, embarrassed, Charlotte felt even younger than her 23 years. Was she really blushing during an important work meeting?

Charlotte willed herself to focus, extending her hand across the desk in what she hoped was a calm, professional gesture. "Charlotte Hastings. It's nice to finally meet you."

His hand enveloped hers. Warm, steady, the briefest brush of callused fingertips against her skin before he released it. He did not smile immediately, but there was a flicker of something – recognition, curiosity – beneath the impassive surface.

"Likewise," he said. "I feel as though we have already been introduced a dozen times over email."

Charlotte laughed lightly, but there was a tightness to it. She felt suddenly very young under his gaze – untried, unpolished in ways that her carefully chosen outfit and resume couldn't disguise.

"Hopefully the real version of me is slightly less frantic than the email version," she said, forcing a little ease into her voice.

The corner of his mouth lifted – not quite a smile, but something close.

"You strike me as someone who handles pressure well."

It was not flirtation. It was something rarer: a genuine compliment, offered without embellishment.

Before she could think of a clever response, Ivy appeared at her side, handing off a neatly bound folder without missing a beat.

"Call me if you need backup," she said, winking so subtly only Charlotte would notice.

"Thank you," Charlotte said dryly, shooting her a look as Ivy disappeared with Clementine trotting smugly at her heels.

Jamie opened the file with deliberate, methodical hands. "Do you have a few minutes?" he asked, not assuming, but not uncertain either.

Charlotte nodded. "Of course. I have all the time in the world for you." She cringed, had she really just said that to a client?

As she led him toward the adjoining conference room, she caught Ivy glancing back from across the lobby – smirking the way only a lifelong friend could smirk.

Charlotte shook her head minutely.

Not a chance.

Jamie walked beside her in silence, his long stride unhurried, his presence oddly grounding. She was acutely aware of the space between them – and how very aware he seemed of it, too.

There was nothing flirtatious about him. And, yet, there was nothing indifferent, either. Charlotte wasn't sure what unsettled her more.

The League might challenge her.

This city might test her at every turn.

But for the first time in a long time, Charlotte felt it deep in her bones – she was exactly where she was meant to be.

Chapter 2: October – House Tours

The West Village was doing what it did best – pretending it hadn't been polished within an inch of its life by hedge fund managers and international heiresses. Tree-lined streets twisted like ivy vines, townhouses leaned into each other like old friends sharing secrets, and golden light spilled from tiny bistros packed with beautiful people.

It was the kind of night where the air smelled faintly of roasting garlic and rain on brick, a night so crisp it carried the first bite of winter in its teeth. The cold clung to the cobblestones and curled around the iron railings, sharp and bracing, the kind that made you pull your coat a little tighter and walk a little faster.

It was a far cry from the Upper East Side – the marbled foyers, the white-gloved doormen, the cool, crisp formality of places like Astor House. Down in the Village, everything was looser, cooler, a little messier in a way that felt almost rebellious. Downtown polish wasn't about perfection; it was artistic and abstract, like the Prat alum galleries that spilled far off ideas into the street, wading like a technicolor river straight from Chelsea.

Inside, American Bar was buzzing with its usual October crowd – the kind of place where trust fund babies who cosplayed as venture capitalists donned vintage Levi's and sipped martinis beside Instagram influencers who cared more about filming their food than eating it. Everyone looked just a little too polished, a little too knowing, like they all had somewhere more important to be, but had decided – very casually – not to rush.

Charlotte and Ivy sat tucked into a small round table near the back, sharing a chopped Caesar salad – the dressing added a kick of spice and it hit just right for this cold, autumn night – and a plate of steak frites piled high with crisp, golden shoestring fries. Two espresso martinis glistened in front of them like little dark promises.

Charlotte pushed up the sleeves of her leather blazer—a sharp, oversized piece technically long enough to be worn as a dress, though she'd layered it over a slip just in case. She liked how it felt: polished but not stuffy, exactly the kind of armor Manhattan demanded.

Across the table, Ivy lounged back effortlessly in high-waisted Khaite jeans, a black cropped top, and tiny kitten heels that made her look like she'd just wandered in off a Vogue street style shoot. Of course she hadn't even brushed her hair, and somehow it still gleamed under the bar's muted lights.

Charlotte speared a crouton with her fork and leaned back against the butter-soft leather banquette, letting out a long, theatrical sigh.

"I feel like I've aged a decade in the past month," she said, half-laughing. "September was... a lot."

Ivy grinned and stole a fry. "Well, you're still vertical. That's something."

Charlotte smiled, but before she could respond, her phone buzzed against the table.

She glanced down—and immediately felt her stomach tighten.

Jamie Harrison.

Of course.

The message was brief, clipped, utterly devoid of pleasantries:

Need updated measurements and historical comps by Monday morning meeting. Include photo documentation from both appraisers and curators' sides. Thx.

Charlotte stared at it, fighting the sudden, ridiculous urge to throw her phone into her half-empty martini.

"Work?" Ivy asked, sipping her drink.

"Yeah," Charlotte said, setting the phone down a little harder than necessary. "Jamie Harrison. Again."

Ivy raised an eyebrow, amused. "Our brooding historic preservationist strikes."

Charlotte let out a breath, trying to shake off the rising tension.

"It's just... he's so —" She broke off, searching for the right word. "Demanding. Incredibly precise. And somehow manages to make every single request sound like an order from God."

Ivy laughed. "Tall, broody, bossy. Your kryptonite."

Charlotte ignored her. Mostly.

She swirled her martini absentmindedly, watching the thin foam ripple.

"The meeting the other day," she said, her voice dropping slightly, "was so much more... professional than I wanted it to be."

She cringed even as she said it – wanted it to be? She barely knew him. It was work.

But still. There had been this flicker of something – this brief, electric moment when their eyes had caught across the conference table, when it had felt like maybe he saw her. Not just the junior staffer taking notes. Her.

And then he'd spent the next hour discussing architectural preservation codes and municipal zoning regulations in a tone so dry that it could have started a drought.

Charlotte sighed again and leaned back, bumping her Bottega bag with the heel of her boot.

"It's not just Jamie," she added. "It's everything. Sotheby's deadlines, House Tours planning, endless committee meetings... I feel like I'm spinning."

Charlotte pushed a fry around her plate, shaking her head.

"You know Sotheby's bought the Breuer Building this summer, right?" she said. "The big Brutalist slab on Madison and 75th? Concrete stacked like an angry sculpture project. It used to be the Whitney, then the Met, then the Frick borrowed it. Now it's ours. A cool hundred million later."

Ivy whistled low. "No pressure."

Charlotte laughed under her breath.

"We're working with Jamie's firm to do a 'sensitive adaptation.' The interiors just got landmarked, so we basically have to preserve everything while still adapting it into a functioning auction space. No mistakes. No breathing too hard on the walls."

"And Jamie's the preservation sheriff?" Ivy teased.

"Basically," Charlotte said. "He's overseeing the historic compliance side, working with the architects, the city, the preservation boards. And, unfortunately, me."

Ivy raised her glass. "Here's to humble stewardship."

They clinked glasses.

But even as she laughed, Charlotte felt the weight of Jamie's text lingering at the back of her mind – sharp, serious, impossible to ignore.

Perfectly professional. Maddeningly handsome. Entirely too present in her head.

She picked up her phone again and started mentally drafting a response.

Work first. Always work first.

***

The conference room at Sotheby's smelled faintly of old paper, espresso, and lemony furniture polish—the scent of a building trying very hard to scrub away its age without losing its gravitas.

Overhead, the recessed lights buzzed softly, casting pale reflections across the polished oak table. Somewhere down the hall, Charlotte could hear the faint hiss and clatter of the staff cappuccino machine, and farther still – the low, thrumming energy of the auction floors, where fortunes were exchanged over the gleam of oil paintings and the sparkle of estate diamonds.

She perched at one end of the table, laptop open, a yellow legal pad beside it, a sharpened pencil rolling slowly back and forth with every slight bounce of her knee, picking at the slight pills of her pale blue cashmere cardigan.

The leather armrests were cool under her palms, her skin buzzing with caffeine and low-grade anxiety.

Across from her, Jamie Harrison sat – calm, composed, infuriatingly difficult to read.

He wore a navy jacket today, but no tie, the top two buttons of his shirt undone. At the collar, she could see a faint edge of chest hair – just enough to hint at something rugged beneath the otherwise polished exterior.

And he smelled – God, he smelled good. Not the sharp, synthetic fog of department store cologne, but something cleaner, subtler: soap, fresh air, maybe a hint of cedar. The kind of scent that made you think of cool mornings and wood-paneled libraries, not boardrooms and preservation hearings.

Charlotte swallowed hard, trying to stay focused.

She probably shouldn't have spent so much time this morning noticing how good he smelled when they shook hands hello.

But she had.

And now here she was, half-listening, half-trying to will her pulse to calm down.

Jamie flipped through her preliminary report, his dark brows drawn slightly together in concentration. The only sounds were the quiet shuffle of paper and the soft hum of the building breathing around them.

"You're missing documentation on three of the gallery spaces," Jamie said finally, tapping the report with one long finger. His voice was low and controlled—but every word felt weighted, deliberate. "And the archival photographs for the lower-level modifications are incomplete."

Charlotte resisted the urge to squirm.

"I sent a request to the archives last week," she said, forcing her voice steady. "I should have it today."

Jamie raised an eyebrow.

"Should?"

The single syllable dropped between them like a test she hadn't studied for.

Charlotte squared her shoulders.

"You'll have it."

For a moment, he just watched her – no smile, no softness – but something in his gaze felt almost too intent, like he was reading more than just the report in front of him.

Then he gave a small, precise nod.

Her phone buzzed against the table, a persistent vibration. She winced, flipping it over quickly. Why had she not turned it off for such an important client meeting?

It was Avery.

Charlotte – Good Morning! Just a reminder, you are responsible for the final House Tour slot. Thank you again for so graciously volunteering for this very. Important. Job. Remember, House Tours are this Saturday. Confirm it by end of day today.

Charlotte's stomach twisted. The crown jewel of the League's fall fundraiser. Charlotte had bitten off way more than she could chew in an effort to impress Avery and her new committee – and she was coming up completely empty.

Jamie shut the folder with a quiet, decisive sound, leaning back slightly in his chair.

"You look worried," he said, voice mild but alert.

Charlotte tucked a strand of hair behind her ear, forcing a smile.

"It's nothing. Volunteer work."

Jamie didn't move. Just waited.

The hum of the auction floors grew louder in her ears – the steady, murmuring background music of money and art and legacy.

Charlotte sighed, giving in.

"It's the Junior League House Tours," she admitted. "I'm supposed to secure a house for the final stop. It's this Saturday. And... my original contact fell through."

Jamie considered this for a moment, his expression unreadable.

Then, casually, almost like it was an afterthought:

"My grandmother's place is still intact," he said. "Upper East Side. Brownstone. Landmark status. Original Tiffany skylight."

Charlotte blinked.

"You'd let the League tour it?" she asked, half in disbelief.

He shrugged, slow and deliberate.

"She would've liked it," he said simply. "She was a League member once. Back when it meant you spent as much time hammering nails as you did hosting galas."

Charlotte's heart gave a small, inconvenient jolt.

Of course. It wasn't just about being generous. It wasn't just about saving her from disaster.

It was his family's legacy, too.

And he was trusting her with it.

***

By Saturday, the city had turned crisp and golden, the sidewalks edged with the first fallen leaves, and the Upper East Side looked like a postcard someone had forgotten to send.

The Junior League House Tours were, as Avery Sinclair liked to remind everyone, not just a fundraiser – they were a performance. And today, the girls had dressed for the part.

Classic knit sets in soft shades of cream and dove gray, Burberry trenches cinched tightly at the waist, strands of heirloom pearls glinting against collarbones sharp enough to cut glass. The scent of Baccarat Rouge floated through the air in expensive little clouds.

Charlotte tugged her pale trench, lightly scalloped at the hem, a little tighter around herself as the group assembled on Madison Avenue, the morning sun bouncing off the polished limestone townhouses around them.

Between each home, there was a sanctioned champagne stop at some of the city's most iconic, French institutions – La Goulue, Bilboquet, Café Boulud – where flutes of icy Veuve Clicquot appeared the moment a kitten heel crossed the threshold.

By the third stop, the girls were laughing a little too loudly and adjusting their Hermès scarves with tipsy hands. By the fifth, someone had already lost a glove.

Charlotte moved through the day like she was holding her breath, nerves coiled tight in her stomach. The final house – the most important stop – was still a secret to the rest of the group.

Avery, in a pristine cream Max Mara coat and tortoiseshell sunglasses the size of dessert plates, had said nothing after the morning meeting.

Just one arched eyebrow, and a tight, suspicious smile.

Enough rope to hang yourself, Charlotte thought grimly, her block heels clicking smartly across the slate sidewalks.

Finally, as the afternoon sun slanted long across the streets, Avery gathered the group in front of a stately brownstone tucked neatly between two larger, more ostentatious buildings.

The girls hesitated, their chatter dimming.

Even Avery faltered, her perfectly glossed lips parting slightly as she read the polished brass plaque affixed to the wrought-iron gate:

"Former Residence of Emily Harrison — NYJL Sustainer, Descendant of Two U.S. Presidents, Patron of the Arts, Advocate for Women's Suffrage."

For a long moment, there was silence.

Charlotte could almost hear Avery trying to recalibrate her face into something neutral and composed.

She failed spectacularly.

"This..." Avery breathed, sunglasses sliding down her nose an inch, "...is the Emily Harrison residence?"

Charlotte smiled politely, tucking a loose curl behind her ear.

"Yes. She was a member of the League for over fifty years."

Without waiting for further questions, she stepped forward and pushed open the heavy oak door.

Inside, the brownstone was a study in timeless New York elegance. The original parquet floors gleamed under the afternoon light. Massive gilt mirrors lined the hallway, reflecting back the girls' champagne-flushed faces. And everywhere – filling the foyer, curling delicately up the sweeping staircase, perched in porcelain bowls on marble-topped tables – were white orchids.

The flowers filled the air with a light, clean fragrance, a hush of white against the rich dark wood, the soaring ceilings, the stained-glass fanlights.

Charlotte moved through the entryway slowly, almost reverently. It was perfect. More perfect than she'd even dared to hope, it felt like a love letter she'd be dreaming of receiving since the time she was a little girl.

The others filed in behind her, their voices dropping to a reverent murmur. Phones snapped discreet photos – no flash, of course. Someone gasped audibly at the intricate hand-carved moldings.

Charlotte stood just inside the doorway, scanning the foyer for Jamie – already composing the words she would say: Thank you. I owe you everything.

But he wasn't there.

She checked the adjoining rooms—empty, except for a docent hired for the day.

No tall, dark figure leaning against the doorframe.

No quiet smile.

No "You're welcome."

Jamie Harrison had disappeared, leaving only the ghosts of white orchids and the faintest trace of clean cedar air behind him.

Charlotte tucked her hands into the pockets of her coat and smiled to herself, the pride and relief blooming somewhere deep in her chest.

He was impossible.

Infuriating.

Utterly unreadable.

And—maybe—exactly the reason this day was everything it needed to be.

Chapter 3: November – Cotillion

Charlotte slipped through the side entrance of the Astor House, shrugging off the last of the cold as a doorman in a navy uniform held the door for her with a practiced smile. She made her way to the dedicated coatroom – an impossibly dainty space with hand-painted wallpaper of winding blossoms and blooms, a glittering chandelier overhead, and a full-length gilt mirror that made even a rushed outfit check feel vaguely glamorous.

A bottle of Diptyque hand lotion – Fleur de Peau, all soft musk and iris – stood neatly atop a marble-topped side table, as perfectly placed as if it were part of the décor.

She slipped off her cream jacket, smoothing it once before handing it to the attendant, and caught her reflection – a little windblown, a little flushed, but standing tall.

Outside the coatroom, the house unfolded around her in warm, polished layers of history. The front staircase dominated the entrance, sweeping up in a wide, elegant curve that still had the power to make Charlotte's heart flutter. It had been built in 1915, when the townhouse had been the private home of Vincent and Helen Astor – yes, those Astors – the kind of family whose legacy filled textbooks and gossip columns alike.

Charlotte trailed one hand lightly along the smooth mahogany banister as she climbed, remembering the whispered stories – how Vincent had inherited his fortune after his father, John Jacob Astor IV, had gone down with the Titanic. There was something haunting about it – the idea that this staircase, this house, had been born in the aftermath of such unimaginable loss.

Even now, more than a century later, the Astor House seemed to carry the weight of its past like a well-tailored coat – quiet, dignified, and impossibly resilient.

Before heading upstairs, Charlotte slipped into the Pine Room, just off the main hall. It wasn't clubby – no heavy leather or dark paneling here – but, rather, charmingly old-fashioned, like a beloved grandmother's parlor.

Mahogany coffee tables gleamed under the flicker of delicate tea lights. The upholstered love seats, covered in soft chintz and faded floral brocades, invited you to sit, sip, and stay longer than you should.

The air smelled faintly of white lilies and freshly polished wood.

The New York Junior League was famously the only chapter in the country whose clubhouse boasted a functioning bar – a fact recounted by members with a mix of pride and whispered rebellion.

Still, there were rules: no dark liquids allowed – no red wine, no coffee, no cola – nothing that could stain the ivory carpets or the pale silk settees.

The bartender, stationed discreetly behind a modest mahogany sideboard, caught Charlotte's eye as she approached.

"Bubbles?" he asked, already reaching for a chilled bottle in a silver bucket of ice.

Charlotte smiled, feeling a little more herself. "Absolutely."

He poured a pale stream of champagne into a delicate flute and slid it across the bar with practiced ease. Charlotte accepted it with a grateful nod, savoring the cool, crisp effervescence as she took her first sip – the kind of bubbles that lifted the weight of the world off your shoulders, even if just for a moment.

Clutching her glass carefully, Charlotte wove her way back towards the grand staircase, heels muffled by the ancient carpet runner worn thin by generations of polished shoes and whispered ambition.

If she was lucky, she thought, Avery Sinclair would already be too engrossed in Thanksgiving Cotillion planning to notice she was a few minutes late.

But Charlotte had never been particularly lucky when it came to Avery Sinclair.

***

Charlotte slipped into the meeting room as quietly as she could, clutching her delicate champagne flute in one hand and her agenda in the other.

The room was lit by a single antique chandelier, the light dimmed to a soft, flattering glow that made everything – the polished oak conference table, the delicate Queen Anne chairs, the ivory walls with their faded silk panels – feel a little dreamlike. It was the kind of room that seemed frozen in time, as if the Astor House itself was determined to resist the rushing chaos of the world outside.

Charlotte tugged at the hem of her Veronica Beard skirt suit as she slid into a seat near the back, hoping she could melt into the furniture unnoticed.

Avery, poised at the head of the table, caught her entrance immediately. She sat impeccably upright, one French-manicured hand resting lightly on an emerald green leather planner embossed with her initials in discreet gold script. The color – a deep, polished jewel tone – was a subtle nod to the League's signature hue.

With a flick of her pen, Avery called the meeting to order.

"Ladies," she said, her voice smooth and commanding, "first things first – let's give a round of applause to Charlotte for pulling off a spectacular House Tour."

A few polite claps echoed around the room. Bunny Lancaster, glowing in a pink boucle set with matching patent ballet flats, gave a cheerful little wave, her pearl bracelet jingling softly like tiny sleigh bells.

Beside her, Cassandra Chao sat impeccably still, a black cashmere knit dress hugging her willowy frame, an Hermès notebook perched neatly beside her phone. Her dark hair was pulled into a razor-sharp chignon, and the only jewelry she wore was a thin gold Cartier Love bracelet that caught the light every time she flicked through her emails. A hedge fund manager by day, she was known for dismantling quarterly earnings calls and debutante drama with equal precision.

She didn't even glance up, but Charlotte caught the faintest curve of a smirk at the corner of her mouth, like she already knew exactly how the evening – and probably Charlotte's next assignment – would unfold.

Avery smiled, tight and polished.

"Well done," she said, and if there was a slightly grudging note beneath the words, no one commented.

Charlotte smiled back, murmuring a quiet "Thank you," and took a tiny, grateful sip of her champagne, savoring the dry, crisp bubbles.

Avery tapped her pen lightly against her planner, the soft clicking sound slicing through the low hum of side conversations.

"Now," she said briskly, "onto our next event—the Thanksgiving Cotillion."

The room straightened instinctively, chairs shifting forwards a fraction of an inch.

The Cotillion was one of the Junior League's most prestigious traditions – an autumn gala where high school juniors and seniors from the city's best prep schools were formally presented to society. Children of the old guard, old money, and, occasionally, very new money alike.

And for many of the women seated around this table, it was part of the long game – the reason their mothers and grandmothers and great-grandmothers had joined the League in the first place. Because no matter how modern Manhattan liked to pretend to be, certain doors were still easier to open when you had the right names on the right dance cards.

It wasn't just about ballgowns and photographs under chandeliers. It was about alliances. About positioning. About quietly ensuring that legacies stayed intact.

And Charlotte, whether she liked it or not, was about to be put at the center of it.

***

Charlotte stabbed a dumpling with her chopsticks, scowling at it like it had personally offended her.

"Babysitting duty," she said flatly. "Out of all the glamorous assignments, babysitting duty."

Across the small kitchen table, Ivy snorted, nearly choking on her jasmine tea. Clementine, curled up under Ivy's chair in her little knitted sweater, gave a sleepy, disapproving thump of her tail.

"I'm sorry," Ivy said, not sounding remotely sorry. "Mother hen to Manhattan's finest? Sounds exactly like the noble public service they promised you."

Charlotte glared at her, then popped the dumpling into her mouth. It was hot, gingery, delicious — comfort food at its finest — but it did little to soothe her pride.

"Behind the scenes," Charlotte grumbled, reaching for another dumpling. "Running around in kitten heels, fluffing dresses, fixing tiaras, keeping high school seniors from bursting into tears over who danced with who first."

She slumped back against her chair, bumping her knee against the wobbly vintage kitchen table that Ivy refused to replace on principle. Their little apartment was dim and cozy, warmed by the scent of the dumplings and the faint vanilla of Ivy's candle burning on the counter. Outside, November wind rattled the windows, making the whole place feel like a snow globe.

"You're basically Cinderella," Ivy said lightly, twirling her chopsticks. "Except with fewer mice and more Prada."

Charlotte groaned dramatically, letting her head fall back against the chair.

"It gets worse."

Ivy, sensing a good story, leaned forward, her dark hair sliding over her shoulder like silk. "Go on."

Charlotte pulled out her phone and flicked open a text from Avery, thrusting it across the table like evidence at a trial.

"One of the debs I'm assigned to supervise? Jamie Harrison's niece."

Ivy blinked. Once. Twice.

Then, slowly, a wicked grin spread across her face. "Oh, that's... delicious."

Charlotte groaned louder, covering her face with both hands.

"Not only do I have to spend the whole night pinning corsages and making sure no one trips down the grand staircase," she said through her fingers, "I also have to do it while pretending not to notice that Jamie Harrison is somewhere in the room, silently judging me."

Ivy looked delighted. "He's absolutely going to be the hottest chaperone at Cotillion. Bar none."

Charlotte lifted her head just enough to shoot her a withering look. "That's not the point."

"It's exactly the point," Ivy said cheerfully, plucking a shrimp shumai from the carton. "You'll be in a ballgown, trying to herd a bunch of Upper East Side princesses... and Mr. Broody Preservationist will be standing there, probably leaning against a marble column looking all tragic and magnificent."

Charlotte dropped her forehead to the table with a thunk.

"And I'll probably have lipstick on my teeth and a hairpin stabbing me in the scalp," she mumbled into the wood.

Ivy laughed and reached across the table to tousle Charlotte's hair affectionately.

"Maybe he'll rescue you," she said in a mock-swoony voice. "Sweep you off your kitten-heeled feet."

Charlotte sat up, making a face. "More likely he'll make a detailed spreadsheet about my logistical failures."

Clementine let out a soft, conspiratorial woof, like even the dog was in on it.

Charlotte picked up her champagne flute – because of course they had opened champagne for a dumpling dinner; Ivy insisted it was 'balance' – and took a long sip.

"You know what the worst part is?" she said, setting her glass down with a tiny clink.

Ivy raised an eyebrow.

"I already know I'm going to be watching for him the whole night. Like an idiot."

Ivy smirked and clinked her glass against Charlotte's. "Welcome to the club."

***

Charlotte found herself standing in the hushed, carpeted splendor of Bergdorf Goodman's evening salon, blinking against the dizzying glitter of sequins, silk, and chandelier light.

The entire sixth floor felt like it belonged to another planet – one where everyone floated around in heels, spoke in low, expensive-sounding voices, and knew exactly how many fittings it took to make a couture gown look "effortless."

Charlotte tugged at the strap of her tote bag, feeling slightly out of place even in her carefully chosen outfit – dark jeans, a camel wool coat, and a pair of sensible heeled boots. She smoothed her hair, half-expecting a sales associate to appear with a polite but firm "can I help you?" and an assessing glance.

Luckily, she wasn't alone.

Bunny Lancaster stood a few feet away, utterly in her element, twirling in front of a massive gilt mirror. She wore a pale blue cashmere turtleneck and a matching wool mini skirt, the whole look topped with a headband perched just so in her glossy blonde hair. She looked like she had stepped out of a Ralph Lauren holiday campaign.

"I can't believe you found one," Bunny said, practically vibrating with excitement. "Last-minute Cotillion gowns are like unicorns. Or available tables at Polo Bar."

Charlotte laughed, letting some of the tension ease from her shoulders. "It helped that I'm not being presented, just working the event. Lower stakes."

Bunny gave her a scandalized look. "Just working? Charlotte, it's still Cotillion. Everyone will be watching. Especially the mothers."

Charlotte made a face but knew Bunny was right. Just because she wasn't being officially introduced didn't mean she could show up looking like an afterthought. Especially not with Avery Sinclair lurking around, waiting to pounce on any perceived misstep.

A sales associate in sleek black appeared at Charlotte's elbow. "Miss Hastings? Your gown is ready."

Charlotte nodded, and the associate led her towards a private fitting alcove where a single garment bag hung waiting on a brass rail.

Bunny clasped her hands together dramatically. "The reveal! I'm ready."

Charlotte unzipped the bag carefully and pulled back the tissue paper. Inside was a gown that made her heart skip a beat – ivory silk with a hint of pearl sheen, the bodice structured but delicate, with narrow straps that would frame her shoulders just so, and a full skirt that swirled like a whisper when she turned.

It wasn't fussy. It wasn't flashy.

It was quietly stunning—the kind of dress that didn't shout for attention but simply expected it.

Bunny let out a soft, reverent gasp. "You're going to look like a Sargent painting."

Charlotte smiled despite herself, the Frick's "Lady Agnew of Lochnaw" vividly in her mind. "That's the idea."

As she slipped into the fitting room, she caught herself wondering – stupidly, helplessly – what Jamie Harrison would think when he saw her.

Would he even notice?

Or would he look straight through her the way he had that first meeting, cataloging her like another artifact to be handled with gloved hands and careful distance?

Charlotte pulled the gown over her head, smoothing the silk against her waist, and turned slowly to face the mirror.

Under the chandelier light, the dress caught the warm gold tones of the room and seemed almost to glow. She caught sight of herself and paused, the noise of the city momentarily slipping away.

Maybe – just maybe – he wouldn't be able to ignore her this time.

"You need earrings," Bunny declared, already rifling through her purse. "I have extras."

Charlotte laughed, shaking off the thought. "Of course you do."

Minutes later, they were bustling out into the cool, crisp evening, Charlotte balancing the garment bag carefully in her arms like it was spun sugar.

Outside, Fifth Avenue glittered under a fading lavender sky, the first holiday windows already starting to blink to life. The city was slipping into that brief, perfect moment before Thanksgiving, when everything felt possible and a little bit magic.

Charlotte exhaled a long, frosty breath into the evening air.

One more day until Cotillion.

One more night of pretending she wasn't about to run headfirst into Jamie Harrison all over again.

And this time, she wouldn't be hidden in the background.

She would be front and center, whether she liked it or not.

***

The Park Plaza had been polished within an inch of its life, every chandelier blazing, every velvet-draped entrance arranged with precision. A thousand tiny reflections winked off crystal glassware, gold-plated flatware, and the immaculate white orchids that tumbled from towering centerpieces like waterfalls.

It was, in short, exactly what a Junior League Cotillion should be.

Outside the grand ballroom, Charlotte stood in a cramped backstage corridor that smelled faintly of hairspray, perfume, and nerves, clutching a sewing kit in one hand and a clipboard in the other.

Somehow, despite her best efforts, she had been absorbed into the volunteer force behind the event: wrangling debutantes, calming flustered mothers, smoothing out last-minute gown disasters. Less fairy tale, more stage manager.

She adjusted the earpiece that linked her to the front-of-house coordinators (yes, there was an earpiece – this was New York, after all) and hurried down the line of debutantes lined up like perfectly coiffed dominoes.

"Breathe," she whispered to a girl whose white gloves trembled slightly at the fingertips. "You look beautiful."

The girl gave a watery smile, and Charlotte tugged the hem of her dress straight before moving on.

Back here, the world was a blur of white satin, stiff tulle, pearls, and proud mothers in jewel-toned evening gowns. Charlotte dodged a beaded train, side-stepped a collapsing hairdo emergency, and handed off a tissue with the swift efficiency of someone who had worked two auction previews in the same day.

"You're a miracle," a frazzled committee chair murmured as Charlotte pinned a slipping sash seconds before the girl was announced.

Charlotte smiled tightly. She was exhausted, slightly sweaty, and seriously questioning her life choices – but at least no one had tripped yet.

She glanced down at herself – the ivory silk gown she'd collected from Bergdorf's hugged her frame perfectly, the skirt falling in a graceful sweep to the floor. Her hair was pinned back in a soft chignon, a few tendrils artfully escaping around her face. Diamond studs winked at her ears.

She didn't exactly blend in, but she didn't feel out of place either.

And then, somehow, she sensed him before she saw him.

Jamie Harrison.

He stepped through the ballroom doors like he'd been painted there by an artist with a very clear agenda – Devastating in full white tie, the starched shirt and black tailcoat cutting a severe, almost archaic figure against the soft glitter of the room.

The kind of man you noticed.

The kind of man you felt noticing you.

Charlotte's heart thudded against her ribs in a wildly unprofessional way.

For a moment, he didn't see her – he was speaking with one of the event organizers, his mouth set in that serious, slightly wry line she recognized all too well. But then his eyes flicked up, scanning the room.

And found her.

Something in his expression shifted – just a fraction, but it was enough. Enough to make her skin prickle under the silk of her gown.

He crossed the distance between them in a few long strides, pausing just in front of her.

"You're not..." he started, then trailed off, something flickering across his face. He looked her up and down, not with the hungry gaze she'd fended off at countless cocktail parties, but with something else. Something quieter. Deeper.

"You look..." Jamie paused again, as if selecting each word with care.

"...exceedingly well suited to the room."

Charlotte blinked, startled – and then, before she could find something clever to say, he offered his hand.

A silent invitation.

She slid her hand into his, feeling the warm, calloused strength of his fingers closing around hers.

Without another word, he led her onto the dance floor.

The orchestra struck up a waltz, rich and full, and Jamie caught her waist with one steady hand, pulling her into position as if it were the most natural thing in the world.

His hand rested lightly against the small of her back – formal, proper, and yet somehow impossibly intimate. Charlotte barely breathed as he guided her into the first sweeping turn.

Their bodies moved together easily, his steps perfectly aligned with hers, as if they had danced together all their lives instead of only just now.

The satin of her skirt whispered against the polished marble with every turn. The chandeliers above blurred into a kaleidoscope of light. The scent of white orchids – clean, delicate, a little wistful – rose from the centerpieces and wrapped around them like a memory.

Jamie didn't say a word as they danced.

He didn't need to.

The slight pressure of his hand at her waist, the careful precision of his steps, the way he watched her – steadily, almost sternly, as if memorizing her – said everything.

Charlotte tilted her head up, catching his gaze.

She thought she saw something there – a warmth, a tension – but it was gone as quickly as it had come.

The music slowed, drawing the dance to a soft close.

Jamie held her hand a second longer than necessary before releasing her, a rare, almost imperceptible smile tugging at the corner of his mouth.

"You belong to another time," he said, his voice low, almost rough.

Charlotte's breath caught in her throat.

She opened her mouth – she wasn't even sure what she meant to say – but he had already stepped back, offering her the barest inclination of his head.

Before she could stop him, Jamie turned and crossed the floor.

Straight toward Avery Sinclair, who waited near the bar in deep emerald silk, watching them both.

Charlotte stood very still.

The music faded.

The chandeliers hummed.

And somewhere deep inside her, something else – the fragile, foolish hope she hadn't even realized she'd been carrying – cracked.

Chapter 4: December – Winter Ball

The weeks leading up to Winter Ball (colloquially know as Junior League Prom) blurred into a flurry of twelve-hour workdays, last-minute committee commitments, and a personal embargo on all things remotely romantic.

Charlotte threw herself into Sotheby's projects with ruthless precision. She was at her desk before sunrise, her oat milk latte balanced precariously between stacks of appraisal reports and glossy exhibition catalogs. If heartbreak had a uniform, Charlotte's was structured wool blazers, pointed heels, and a lipstick sharp enough to slice through any lingering hope.

Outside, the city was getting dressed for the holidays. Shop windows along Madison Avenue bloomed with velvet gowns, towering nutcrackers, and snowy tableaux so perfect they felt like dreams you could step into.

Bergdorf's glittered like a bejeweled music box, every window a different fantasy: crystal swans, gilt mirrors, paper flowers bigger than her head. Fifth Avenue was ablaze with fairy lights, the sidewalks lined with shoppers wrapped in cashmere and holiday cheer.

New York shimmered.

And Charlotte buried herself in spreadsheets, historic landmark regulations, and auction inventories, refusing to look up.

When she had to interface with Jamie Harrison – which, of course, was a daily occurrence – she met him with cool, polite professionalism.

No lingering glances.

No unnecessary small talk.

No visible cracks in the armor she had painstakingly assembled.

If Jamie noticed the shift, he didn't show it. He sat across conference tables and beside architectural blueprints, his gaze steady but unreadable, and Charlotte pretended she didn't catch the way his eyes sometimes lingered a second too long.

She buried herself in zoning regulations and compliance reports. She memorized historical preservation codes like they were prayers.

Because work was safe.

Work didn't make you dream about a man who smelled like cedarwood and old paper and looked at you like you were both a puzzle and the solution all in one.

***

Monday morning came cold and clear, the kind of morning where the air cut straight through your coat and left your lungs sparkling.

Charlotte slipped into the third-floor conference room at Sotheby's, cradling a fresh cappuccino in one hand and a leather portfolio in the other. Her navy dress was simple and sharp, belted neatly at the waist, her heels clicking smartly against the polished wood floors.

She had just opened her laptop when the door creaked open again.

Jamie stepped inside, bringing the cold with him.

He didn't bother to brush the fine dusting of snow from the shoulders of his charcoal coat. Tiny crystals clung stubbornly to the dark wool – and to the rough line of his ever-present five o'clock shadow, catching there like fragile silver threads.

He shrugged the coat off and slung it over the back of his chair, sleeves already pushed up to reveal the strong line of his forearms, a scuffed watch peeking out from under the cuff.

Without preamble, he spread a set of floor plans across the table, the crisp edges whispering against the oak.

"We need final sign-off from the Landmark Preservation Commission before any structural work begins on the stairwell," Jamie said, his voice low and even.

Charlotte clicked open her notes, meeting his gaze without flinching.

"The main concern is safeguarding the Dwellings installation."

Jamie's eyes flicked up – just briefly – but enough to make her pulse jump.

"Charles Simonds," Charlotte continued, keeping her voice steady. "His miniature clay village tucked into the second-floor stairwell niche. Commissioned by the Whitney in 1981. Materials: clay, sand, sticks, wood, plaster, cloth, chicken wire."

A ghost of a smile crossed Jamie's mouth.

"You've been doing your homework."

Charlotte tapped her pen lightly against the edge of her portfolio. "If we touch the surrounding masonry — even a hairline shift — the Dwellings could destabilize. I'm coordinating with the archival conservators. During interior work, the niche will be fully sealed. Humidity and temperature monitored hourly."

Jamie leaned back slightly in his chair, studying her like he was fitting together a puzzle only he could see.

"And the two related sculptures across the street?" he asked. "940 Madison?"

Charlotte nodded. "Flagged. Preservation team is documenting them this week. Non-intervention protocol in place."

For a moment, neither of them spoke. Outside, the wind rattled faintly against the windows, a hollow sound.

Charlotte shifted slightly in her seat, catching the familiar brush of the pearl studs at her ears — the simple ones her mother used to wear for Junior League meetings, polished to a soft gleam. A small, steady comfort. A reminder of why she was here.

Jamie set his pen down carefully.

"Good work, Hastings."

He said it with no flourish, no empty courtesy. Just a kind of quiet, contained sincerity that somehow landed harder than any compliment she could remember.

Charlotte only nodded, cool and crisp.

Business. Always business.

Even if, deep down, she felt like the silk thread that had been holding her together all these weeks had just pulled a little tighter.

***

The ferry rocked gently against the harbor dock, ribbons of garland twisted around the gangway rails, tiny white lights blinking against the gray December sky.

Nantucket at Christmas was like stepping into a snow globe. A little weathered around the edges, maybe, but still magical in the way only an island could be once the tourists fled and the locals reclaimed it for themselves.

Charlotte and Ivy tugged their wool coats tighter against the ocean wind as they stepped onto the cobblestone streets. The salt air mixed with the sharper scents of woodsmoke and pine wreaths, and Charlotte felt herself breathe a little easier for the first time in weeks.

Holiday Stroll was tradition. Non-negotiable. And after the month Charlotte had just had, she needed it more than she dared admit.

They piled into Ivy's old Land Rover Defender – its floor still dusted in beach sand from summer – and drove the winding road out towards Sconset.

Ivy's family home sat near the lighthouse, a classic island house weathered to a perfect shade of silver-gray, its robin's egg blue doors gleaming against the muted winter landscape. White trim curled along the eaves like lace, and a wreath made of driftwood and seashells hung crookedly on the front gate.

It wasn't grand in the glossy magazine sense. It was better – real, lived-in, and beloved.

They dropped their bags inside – Charlotte's usual room still papered in soft blue toile, Ivy's under the sloped eaves with a window overlooking the sea – and headed back into town.

Main Street was already alive, the storefronts decked in wreaths the size of wagon wheels, every windowpane frosted with hand-painted snowflakes. The whaling museum stood at the heart of it all, its wide brick façade strung with evergreen garlands. Inside, the Festival of Trees was in full swing – a dizzying, twinkling display of dozens of Christmas trees, each one decorated by a local business.

They wandered slowly, admiring the details – Bartlett's Farm's tree dripping with tiny corn husk angels, the Brewery's tree wrapped in hops vines, the library's decked in miniature book ornaments, Cru's shimmering with pearly oyster shells and navy velvet ribbons.

Charlotte paused in front of a tree dusted in antique glass baubles, a simple gold star perched at the top.

"It's almost too much," she said, smiling despite herself. "Like they bottled Christmas Eve and shook it over the whole island."

Ivy grinned and looped her arm through Charlotte's. "Good. You needed some sparkle back in your life."

They moved deeper into the museum, their steps muffled by the wide-planked floors. Children's laughter echoed through the galleries, and somewhere upstairs a string quartet played a shy, meandering version of Have Yourself a Merry Little Christmas.

They ended up at a quiet overlook near a window, the harbor gray and still beyond the glass. Ivy nudged her gently.

"All right," she said. "Spill. You've been weird ever since Thanksgiving."

Charlotte wrapped her mittened hands tighter around her coffee, pretending to watch the gulls dipping over the water.

"I don't know," she said finally. "At Cotillion — I saw Jamie and Avery. Talking."

Ivy raised a brow. "Talking isn't exactly a crime."

"It wasn't just talking," Charlotte insisted, her voice low. "It felt — familiar. Like they knew each other better than I thought."

Ivy gave a noncommittal shrug. "You sure you're not reading into it? Cotillion's a high-stakes night. Tuxedos, champagne, chandeliers — It does weird things to people's heads."

Charlotte laughed under her breath, a small, brittle sound.

"Maybe," she said. "Maybe I'm just being ridiculous."

"You're not ridiculous," Ivy said firmly. "You're human. You like him. That's allowed."

Charlotte pressed her lips together, staring out at the shifting gray of the harbor.

"I just don't want to get it wrong," she said quietly. "I don't want to be blindsided."

Ivy linked their arms and gave a little tug, steering her back towards the museum's main hall, where the Christmas trees twinkled and the air smelled like cinnamon and evergreen.

"You won't," Ivy said. "And even if you do – you'll survive. You always do."

***

Later that afternoon, after one too many gingerbread lattes and a charitable donation to the local bookstore's entire inventory, Ivy tugged Charlotte down a side street lined with tiny boutiques strung in white lights.

"Enough moping," Ivy declared, linking their arms. "We're getting you a dress for Winter Ball."

Charlotte laughed, half-protesting. "We have dresses. We have too many dresses."

"You have closet panic and emotional baggage," Ivy corrected. "There's a difference. And you haven't even bothered to pick anything out yet. Winter Ball is, like, a week away."

Charlotte sighed, her boots crunching on the salt-dusted cobblestones. She had barely been able to think about Winter Ball, let alone prepare for it. She'd told herself she was too busy. But really, she hadn't wanted to picture the night – the chandeliers, the music – because she couldn't stop imagining who might already be waiting there with someone else.

Still, she let Ivy steer her across Main Street toward the island's most iconic stop – Murray's Toggery Shop.

The old red-and-white awning flapped gently in the cold breeze, and the brass bell chimed as they slipped inside. The store smelled like worn leather, cedar, and clean cotton – like history itself.

Murray's wasn't just any store. It was the store. The birthplace of Nantucket Reds – the faded, sun-bleached canvas pants worn by fishermen, sailors, and generations of locals who understood that style here wasn't loud, it was lived-in. Inspired by the weathered reds of Brittany's coastal fishermen, the pants had become a local legend, and Murray's remained the only place legally allowed to sell authentic ones.

Ivy headed straight for the holiday section tucked beside the men's racks of pastel polos and cable-knit sweaters.

A few evening dresses hung on a circular rack dusted with pine garland – jewel-toned velvets, airy chiffons, classic satins.

Charlotte trailed her fingers along the hangers, heart not really in it – until she saw it.

Simple. Elegant. Red.

Nantucket Red.

Not the casual, sun-faded cotton of the island's famous pants, but something bolder, richer – the same spirit, distilled into silk. A true, fearless red that carried a quiet kind of confidence. The gown was cut from heavy silk, the bodice fitted with a subtle sweetheart neckline and delicate straps, the skirt full but clean, swishing dramatically as she lifted it from the rack.

Ivy clapped her hands in delight. "Oh, that's it. That's the dress."

Charlotte hesitated, biting her lip. It wasn't what she would normally pick. She usually stayed safe – champagne, dove gray, navy. But something about it – the fearless sweep of the skirt, the way it caught the last of the winter light – felt exactly right.

Holiday spirits – real, actual, stubborn ones – lifted somewhere inside her chest.

"Okay," she said, smiling for the first real time in days. "Let's do it."

***

The ballroom at Casa Cipriani glittered like a dream.

Golden light spilled from low-slung chandeliers, casting a warm glow over the crowd of tuxedos and evening gowns that shimmered like oil paintings come to life. Strings of tiny white lights wove through garlands of pine and ivy, curling along the wrought iron balconies and polished marble floors.

Charlotte stood just inside the entrance, clutching her invitation, her heart pounding hard against her ribs – like a bird trapped inside a too-small cage.

Her dress floated around her ankles with every step, showing off her delicate Loeffler Randal sandals. The full skirt moved like a sigh against the floor, the fitted bodice a quiet nod to the kind of effortless glamour she didn't always feel she could claim.

Tonight, though, she had tried.

Her hair was swept back in a loose, low chignon. Pearl studs glinted softly at her ears. She had even let Bunny convince her to borrow her vintage Dior Lady Bag (named for Lady Di, of course).

Avery Sinclair swept past her, deep in conversation with a group of other committee chairs, her emerald-green satin gown catching the light with every sharp turn of her head. She looked like the personification of Christmas itself – Polished, commanding, untouchable.

Charlotte inhaled deeply and moved further into the room, weaving her way through glittering couples and waiters balancing trays of champagne flutes.

She spotted a few familiar faces – Bunny, laughing too loudly in a corner; Cassandra, cool and composed with a glass of something clear and expensive in hand – but mostly, the room blurred into color and movement.

Until she saw him.

Jamie.

Standing near the balcony doors, the night stretching out in velvet darkness behind him, he looked impossibly handsome in classic black tie – and he wasn't alone.

The woman beside him was tall and willowy, dressed in a pale blue gown that floated like mist. She leaned in as they spoke, her hand brushing lightly against Jamie's sleeve, laughing at something he said.

It wasn't overtly intimate – no lingering touches, no preening glances. Just… comfortable. Easy. Like they belonged there together.

Charlotte's stomach twisted sharply, the air catching in her throat.

She turned away, focusing hard on the tray of champagne that floated past, willing her heart to slow.

It's fine.

He's allowed to have a date.

You're not his anything.

She found herself drifting towards the balcony doors, desperate for fresh air, the silk of her skirt whispering around her ankles. Her fingers trembled slightly as she reached for the iron handle.

And just as she pushed it open, a flash of light exploded in her peripheral vision.

Paparazzi.

A blur of lenses and shouted questions – and before Charlotte could react, a flashbulb caught her mid-step, the red silk of her gown burning against the dark of the December night.

She stumbled backward, heart hammering. Someone caught her elbow – an older man, distinguished, silver-haired, the kind of guest who probably had a wing named after him at the Met. He chuckled and murmured something polite about the photographers being "overzealous this time of year," steadying her until she found her balance.

Charlotte mumbled her thanks, cheeks burning, and fled back into the relative safety of the ballroom.

She didn't even register Jamie's eyes finding her across the room.

Didn't register the faint furrow between his brows.

All she could think about was getting through the next hour without humiliating herself further.

It wasn't until the next morning that the real disaster struck.

Her phone buzzed violently on the nightstand, far too early for good news. Groggy, Charlotte fumbled for it – and froze.

Page Six: Mystery Socialite Caught Cozying Up to Billionaire at Winter Ball!

There it was.

A photo of her – red dress, dazed expression, caught in the flash – smiling up at the older man who had helped her.

The caption practically dripped with implication.

Charlotte threw the covers over her head and groaned into her pillow.

By noon, Sotheby's had called for a meeting about "appropriate representation at client events."

By two, Avery had sent a bland but razor-sharp text: Hope you're enjoying your fifteen minutes.

By four, the League's rumor mill was whirring at full speed.

She didn't even open Jamie's text when it came through that evening.

She couldn't.

Instead, she stared at the cracked ceiling of her tiny apartment, the December wind rattling against the windows, and wondered.

Had she just been unlucky?

Or had someone been planning it that way all along?

Chapter 5: January – Apres Ski

The conference room at Sotheby's smelled historic – old paper, leather bindings, the faint iron bite of fountain pen ink soaked deep into the grain of the wood. Deals had been made here that had shifted the fortunes of dynasties. Heirloom tiaras saved from pawnshops, Rembrandts spirited quietly between family vaults, Gilded Age mansions sold piece by precious piece.

Outside, Madison Avenue lay locked in the sharp, crystalline chill of January. The city's holiday finery had been stripped away, leaving only bare trees and salt-streaked curbs behind. Even the windows along the avenue – Bergdorf's, Hermès, the Carlyle Hotel – seemed to shimmer a little less brightly, as if exhausted by the season's demands.

Inside, Charlotte Hastings sat perched at the edge of a carved mahogany chair, every muscle drawn tight.

Across the polished table, two senior directors from Sotheby's glanced down at a file that Charlotte already knew by heart. Photographs from the Winter Ball, a blurred flashbulb moment twisted into something careless. The Page Six headline was printed at the top of the dossier in mocking, tabloid-bold letters.

She adjusted the sleeves of her navy crepe dress, smoothing invisible wrinkles, the movement stiff and mechanical. Her pearl studs gleamed softly at her ears, a quiet echo of the formality around her.

On the far side of the room, a small arrangement of white orchids stood on a sideboard – pristine and almost too delicate for the heavy-paneled space. Charlotte found herself staring at them, focusing hard on the curve of each petal, the impossible neatness of them. It was either that or let herself spiral into the rising, panicked heat prickling at the base of her throat.

"Miss Hastings," one director said, steepling his fingers together. "You understand why you're here?"

Charlotte nodded, her voice caught somewhere behind her ribs.

"This institution," the second director continued, his tone cool but not unkind, "relies on a very particular reputation. We manage more than objects; we steward histories, legacies. Discretion is not just valued – it's required."

Charlotte's heart pounded so loudly she almost missed the soft knock at the door.

The room turned as one.

Barbara Fairchild – in a tailored gray coat and a strand of pearls that seemed to hum with old New York authority – swept inside without waiting for permission. Her entrance alone felt like a shift in atmosphere, the way a church hushes when someone important walks in.

And behind her, tall and rumpled from the cold, his coat still dusted with January snow, was Jamie Harrison.

For a long beat, no one said anything.

Charlotte stared, too stunned to react. She hadn't called anyone.

She hadn't dared.

But Jamie had.

Somehow – maybe through that impossible network of old family ties and whispered favors – Jamie had caught wind of the meeting. And he'd called in Barbara Fairchild, one of the few people who could tilt the scales in a place like Sotheby's with a few well-chosen words.

Barbara gave the directors a slow, deliberate smile that managed to be both charming and unmistakably pointed.

"I believe," she said, her voice smooth as silk, "that there's been a misunderstanding."

Jamie stepped forward, pulling a crisp manila folder from inside his coat and setting it down atop the file on the table — neatly, deliberately, like a final move in a game Charlotte hadn't even known she was playing.

"I was with Miss Hastings at the time in question," he said smoothly, voice low and sure. "In a professional capacity. She was assisting a family acquaintance – an elderly donor to the Whitney – when the photographs were taken. Any implication otherwise is baseless."

Charlotte blinked at him, stunned.

Barbara tilted her head slightly, pearls catching the light.

"In a city like New York," Barbara interjected, "where the circles are small and the memories are long, it's rather important to know who stands with you – and who might be watching."

Her eyes gleamed as she added, "Fortunately, some of us remember what loyalty looks like."

Silence reigned for a beat. Then, reluctantly, the senior director cleared his throat.

"In light of these clarifications," he said, shuffling the papers, "we'll consider the matter closed."

Charlotte's breath left her in a slow, silent rush she didn't even realize she'd been holding.

Barbara and Jamie didn't linger. They offered quick, polite nods, then swept back into the corridor as swiftly as they had arrived, the door swinging shut behind them with a soft, definitive click.

The white orchids caught Charlotte's eye again, swaying slightly in the draft **from the closing door.**

Still perfect.

Still standing.

And, somehow, so was she.

**

The Solidcore studio smelled faintly of eucalyptus and ambition.

Low blue lighting pulsed over rows of sleek Pilates reformers, each one gleaming like a machine of beautifully disguised torture.

A massive neon sign glowed at the back of the room – STRONGER THAN YESTERDAY – a silent dare to anyone who thought they might be here for a casual stretch, and a thinly veiled threat to those who had been lazily missing their classes.

Charlotte adjusted the straps on her Alo Yoga matching set – a muted dove gray that Ivy had convinced her was "neutral, chic, and sweat-proof" – hint, it wasn't – and tucked her grippy socks firmly into place.

Around her, the committee girls were busy snapping ponytails into high, tight buns and adjusting the waistbands of their matching Alo sets in various shades of winter white, sage, and blush pink.

Avery Sinclair, naturally, looked like a brand ambassador. Her deep emerald green leggings and matching cropped jacket pristine, her high, sleek ponytail unmoving even as she lunged into a few effortless warm-up squats. She looked like money itself had gone to Pilates – the epitome of the UES dream.

Charlotte inhaled slowly, steeling herself.

Forty-five minutes later, she wasn't sure if she could feel her own legs.

The instructor, a terrifyingly chipper brunette with the build of a ballet dancer and the voice of a drill sergeant, barked out another endless plank series, and Charlotte gritted her teeth, refusing to be the first to collapse onto the machine like a beached whale.

Every muscle in her body trembled.

The only thing more exhausting than holding a plank for eternity was pretending not to care who noticed if you failed. This was all set against a bubbly set of pop music and house – who knew the best DJ in the whole City was a Pilates instructor.

When it was finally, mercifully over, Charlotte wiped down her machine, hands still shaking slightly, and made her way towards the lobby.

At the coat rack, the women bundled into their Moncler puffers and Canada Goose parkas, slipping into shearling-lined boots and draping wool scarves over their shoulders with languid, post-workout glamour.

Cheery, botoxed faces beamed at each other in the mirror-lined lobby, all perfectly plumped lips and air-kissed goodbyes, like no one had just spent fifty minutes fighting for their life on a Pilates machine.

Avery lingered by the mirror, zipping her parka with deliberate grace.

"So," she said, voice honey-sweet, "heard you had a little… excitement at Winter Ball."

Charlotte smiled lightly, slipping into her own coat.

"I'd call it more of a misunderstanding."

Avery's perfectly sculpted brows arched. "Mmm. Well. Glad to hear Sotheby's didn't hold it against you."

Charlotte shrugged, casual, calm. "People who matter know the difference."

Cassandra Chao, lounging nearby in oversized Celine sunglasses, lifted her coffee cup in a small, lazy toast.

Avery's smile tightened a fraction before she turned to fuss with her phone.

As Charlotte adjusted the collar of her coat, she caught Cassandra's reflection in the mirror – a ghost of a smirk flashing across her otherwise unreadable face – before she pushed open the studio door and disappeared into the bright January afternoon.

The shift was subtle.

But Charlotte felt it all the same.

The tide was turning.

And this time, she was riding it.

***

The studio smelled like charcoal dust and melting wax.

Charlotte perched stiffly at an old wooden easel, the battered stool beneath her creaking ominously every time she shifted. All around her, half-finished sketches of torsos, shoulders, and backs glowed under the flicker of scattered candelabras, their wax pooling like molten rivers onto the concrete floor.

She wasn't sure what she had expected when Ivy had insisted she come along to her "Wednesday night sanity check."

Certainly not... this.

The model, a perfectly proportioned man with the resigned air of someone very used to being stared at, shifted into a new pose atop the dais, stretching one arm languidly overhead.

Charlotte's charcoal skittered embarrassingly across her page.

"This feels illegal," she whispered to Ivy, who sat cross-legged beside her, sketching with the lazy precision of someone completely unfazed by nudity – or life, for that matter.

"It's art," Ivy said serenely, shading a deft line along the curve of a shoulder blade. "Don't be so provincial. You're practically a New Yorker now."

Charlotte smirked, wiping the side of her palm across her paper and only managing to smear charcoal even further.

Her drawing looked like a haunted scarecrow. Perfect.

Outside, the January night pressed against the frosted windows, muffling the usual sounds of the city into something quieter, dreamlike. The distant honk of a cab, the soft shuffle of boots over slush, even the low hum of traffic – all muted by the thick hush of new snow.

Inside, the room crackled with low conversation and the scratch of charcoal on thick paper. Shadows danced across the exposed brick walls, throwing elongated silhouettes of the model and the students alike, as if they were part of some strange, secret ritual.

"So," Ivy said casually, not looking up from her drawing, "are you ready for Après Ski?"

Charlotte groaned under her breath and set her charcoal down with a soft clink.

"Define ready," she muttered. "I have a deep desire to not be trapped at another League event where everyone keeps whispering behind their champagne glasses."

Ivy laughed, flicking a lock of hair out of her eyes. "Perfect. You'll fit right in. Everyone just wants to wear designer goggles, sip spiked hot cocoa, and take Instagram photos. It's harmless."

"Except for the fake gondola," Charlotte said darkly. "I saw it on the committee planning email. It's a kissing booth. For charity. That can only end badly."

Ivy's head snapped up, her eyes alight with mischief.

"Wait—an actual kissing booth? Like high school carnival kissing booth?"

Charlotte nodded grimly. "Decorated to look like a gondola. Alpine chic, they said. Alpine disaster, I say."

"You," Ivy said, tapping her charcoal thoughtfully against her sketchpad, "have a truly tragic lack of whimsy."

Charlotte picked up her pencil again, sketching a wobbly line that was supposed to be a thigh but looked more like an overly ambitious baguette.

"I have enough whimsy," she said dryly. "Just... selective deployment."

"Well, start deploying," Ivy said, stretching her arms overhead in a lazy arc. "You survived Cotillion. You survived Winter Ball. Après Ski will be a cakewalk. Plus, you have a killer jacket."

Charlotte sighed, thinking of the vintage Moncler she'd borrowed from Ivy's cavernous coat closet – a glossy black puffer cinched at the waist, just retro enough to feel cool without trying too hard.

And really, what could go wrong at a charity event designed by women who never missed a barre class or a blowout appointment?

Maybe it wouldn't be so bad.

Maybe.

The model shifted again, settling into a deep twist that left very little to the imagination.

Charlotte promptly dropped her charcoal stick with a loud clatter that echoed embarrassingly across the room.

Ivy grinned wickedly, reaching for another sheet of paper. "Selective deployment, huh?"

Charlotte only laughed, the tight knot in her chest loosening a fraction for the first time all day.

Because maybe, just maybe, surviving the Winter Ball scandal had left her tougher.

Maybe the cold couldn't sting as much when you were already a little frozen over inside.

Maybe this time, she could actually enjoy herself, no heartstrings attached.

***

The Astor House had been transformed.

Gone were the polished oak floors and heirloom rugs. Tonight, the grand front room was strewn with faux snow, silver birch branches, and enough twinkle lights to rival a small ski village.

White faux-fur throws draped over love seats, and a DJ in a Fair Isle sweater spun a mix of 80's ski-lodge anthems and holiday classics remixed with a heavy bassline.

Charlotte paused just inside the entrance, adjusting the vintage Moncler jacket cinched tightly at her waist. Underneath, she wore a fitted cashmere turtleneck and cream ski pants tucked neatly into knee-high boots. Her hair was braided back in a low, glossy knot, her cheeks already pink from the bite of the January air.

The whole effect was deliberate. Chic but not flashy, timeless but not trying too hard. She'd promised herself – no mistakes tonight. No whispers. No photos. Just survival.

The League members had outdone themselves. Groups of women in matching Perfect Moment après-ski sets and high-gloss puffer vests clutched spiked hot chocolates in paper cups embossed with tiny gold snowflakes. A few brave souls had already posed inside the infamous "Gondola Kissing Booth" – an elaborate setup complete with faux-wood siding, sheepskin throws, and a little plaque that read "Kisses for a Cause."

At the far end of the room, the bar boasted a towering ice luge, carved playfully into the looping initials NYJL – a frosted sculpture that caught and fractured the warm light like a prism. Champagne and Aperol spritzes slid down the frozen curves into delicate coupe glasses, to the squealing delight of a few girls who had clearly lost all fear of brain freeze.

Charlotte caught a glimpse of Avery Sinclair sweeping past the bar in a fitted emerald ski jacket and white leather leggings, her glossy hair gleaming under the chandeliers. Avery didn't even spare the ice luge a glance – pretending, with well-practiced ease, that it simply didn't exist – while somehow still managing to look like she owned the room.

Charlotte smiled despite herself. It was over-the-top. It was ridiculous.

It was exactly what she needed.

***

Charlotte was halfway through her second cautious sip of champagne when she felt a tug at her elbow.

"Come on," Bunny Lancaster said, materializing at her side in a white fur-trimmed ski jacket that was definitely more après than ski. Her cheeks were flushed pink from the heat and excitement, a glass of something pink and sparkling wobbling precariously in her free hand.

Charlotte raised an eyebrow. "Come on where?"

Bunny leaned in conspiratorially, her voice dropping to a whisper. "To the gondola booth, obviously. It's for charity. One kiss, one donation."

Charlotte nearly choked on her drink. "Bunny, absolutely not."

Bunny giggled, tugging her insistently toward the faux gondola set up near the back of the room. The booth was absurdly over-the-top. A life-sized gondola lift car, painted in glossy red and white, nestled beneath a spray of fake pine boughs and twinkle lights. Inside, a tufted velvet bench waited under a string of mistletoe so enormous it could have qualified as a biological weapon.

"It's harmless!" Bunny chirped, flashing a bright, not-at-all-innocent smile. "You just sit. Maybe kiss someone's cheek. It's for charity."

Charlotte dug her heels into the polished parquet floor. "Bunny—"

But Bunny was stronger than she looked (Pilates, probably) and before Charlotte could properly resist, she was being propelled forward and bundled into the gondola car with a gentle but firm shove.

The door snapped shut behind her with an ominous click.

Charlotte exhaled a long, suffering breath – and then froze.

Because someone else was already sliding into the gondola, his tall frame ducking under the low ceiling, dark hair tousled, navy ski jacket unzipped just enough to reveal the starched white collar of his shirt.

Jamie Harrison.

Charlotte's mouth went completely dry.

For a moment, they simply stared at each other, the world narrowing to the absurd little cabin, the soft scrape of his boots against the metal floor, the heavy, humming silence.

Then the gondola shuddered slightly as it locked into place.

Outside, Bunny's giggles – and someone else's "aww!" – filtered through the thin plastic windows.

Charlotte opened her mouth to say something – anything – but Jamie beat her to it.

"I swear," he said dryly, "I had no part in this."

Charlotte gave a strangled laugh, pressing the back of her head lightly against the velvet bench cushion. "Of course not," she muttered. "That would require a sense of humor."

Something flickered in Jamie's expression, the barest ghost of a smile.

The gondola gave a slight, creaky sway, nudging them a fraction closer together.

Outside, the party raged on. Music pulsing, corks popping, heels clacking on polished floors. In here, it was still. Too still.

"So," Jamie said after a moment, voice low and rough around the edges, "are you going to accuse me of being engaged to my cousin?"

Charlotte turned sharply towards him, mortified heat flooding her cheeks. "She was very pretty," she said defensively, then winced. "I mean—"

Jamie leaned back slightly, arms draped casually along the back of the seat. "Amelia. Visiting from London. Fundraising for her children's literacy foundation."

He paused, his gaze steady and a little too perceptive.

"And my second cousin. Once removed."

Charlotte closed her eyes briefly, wishing she could sink through the floor.

The gondola swayed again, and Charlotte, thrown slightly off balance, ended up closer to him than she intended – close enough to feel the low, steady heat radiating off his body; close enough to notice the faint scent of cedar still clinging to his jacket.

For a long moment, neither of them moved.

Charlotte stared down at the tiny scratch on her leather phone case – emblazoned with her initials CH – willing herself not to do anything idiotic.

"I thought I had it figured out," she said softly, the words slipping out before she could stop them. "I thought... maybe you and Avery—"

Jamie's mouth tightened slightly. Not angry. Something else. Sadness, maybe. Regret.

"Avery's not the story you think she is," he said after a beat. "Stop looking for things that aren't there."

Charlotte risked a glance up at him, surprised by the raw honesty in his voice.

The gondola door rattled loudly, a clumsy jolt as someone fumbled with the latch from the outside.

Charlotte startled, the moment breaking like a dropped champagne flute.

Seconds later, Bunny's laughing face appeared through the little window, cheeks pink with cold and champagne. "Technical malfunction!" she called brightly. "Hang tight!"

Jamie exhaled a rough breath and leaned his head back against the seat, eyes closing briefly as if steeling himself.

Charlotte sat very, very still, hands clasped in her lap, heart hammering so loudly she was certain he could hear it.

Another minute. Maybe two.

And then the door finally swung open with a loud, freeing creak.

Jamie stood first, offering his hand to help her out. His palm was warm, steady, fingers curling instinctively around hers for the briefest moment.

Charlotte didn't breathe until they were back on solid ground.

The party swallowed them both up again almost immediately – laughing girls in Fair Isle sweaters, guys in ski jackets and beanies jostling for cocktails – but Charlotte felt different.

Changed.

As she drifted towards the bar, reaching blindly for another champagne flute, she caught herself smiling – a small, secret smile no one else could see.

Maybe her heart wasn't such a lost cause after all.

Maybe, just maybe, the cage door was starting to creak open.

Chapter 6: February – Galentine's Day

Overnight, the city had sprouted pink hearts like wildflowers pushing up through frostbitten ground. They clung stubbornly to café windows and bakery doors, fluttered from lampposts, and winked from behind the frosted glass of Madison Avenue storefronts. Against the endless gray of February – bare trees, slush-smeared curbs, salt-streaked cars – they looked almost defiant.

Small, bright acts of hope.

Charlotte tugged her red cashmere scarf tighter around her neck, her breath clouding in the sharp morning air as she made her way towards Ladurée.

Inside, pastel towers of macarons glittered under soft gold lighting, and heart-shaped boxes tied with velvet ribbons filled the windows, looking almost absurdly cheerful against the slate-colored sky.

The door swung open just as she reached for it.

Jamie stepped out, holding it lightly with one gloved hand. His hair was damp from the snow, tiny crystals clinging to the rough line of his jaw where stubble shadowed his skin.

For a second, they both hesitated.

"Morning," he said, voice low.

"Morning," Charlotte replied, forcing her mouth into something resembling a smile as she slipped inside.

The warmth of the bakery hit her immediately – vanilla, butter, and strong coffee. She pulled off her gloves slowly, giving herself a moment to breathe.

Behind the counter, pistachio croissants – pistak-ee-oo, she thought, remembering Ivy's well-traveled correction – glimmered under glass domes.

It was technically their Monday morning meeting.

But instead of the cold polish of Sotheby's conference rooms, Jamie had suggested grabbing coffee today. A small, unexpected change. A crack in the pattern.

Charlotte clung to it, careful not to hope too much.

Jamie ordered for them – for himself a black coffee, for her an oat milk latte – and found a quiet table by the window, the city streaming past in muted grays and flashes of pink.

He set down his coffee with the kind of precision he applied to everything else. No fidgeting, no unnecessary movement.

Charlotte stirred her latte once, twice, the tiny silver spoon clicking softly against the porcelain.

She could still feel the ghost of Après Ski between them – the low hum of music, the warm crush of bodies, the way his hand had brushed hers in the dark of that ridiculous gondola. The moment had hovered, fragile and unspoken.

But Jamie didn't bring it up. Instead, he set down a thick folder between them. The cover was unmarked, but Charlotte recognized it instantly: Breuer building renovation plans.

He tapped a finger against it absently.

"They finalized the restoration guidelines," he said. "We're preserving everything that matters — concrete walls, bluestone floors, bronze fixtures, the original wood handrails. Not polishing the life out of it. Just targeted work where it's needed."

Charlotte traced the rim of her coffee cup slowly.

"And the lobby?"

Jamie nodded.

"Circulation's better. They pulled out all the junk that got added after '66. It'll breathe again — the way that Breuer meant it to. Honest materials, clean lines. No clutter, no gimmicks. Just the building, telling its own story."

There was a softness to his voice when he said it.

A kind of reverence she didn't usually hear from him.

Charlotte leaned back slightly, studying him over the rim of her cup.

"Not everything old needs to be torn down to start over," he said quietly, almost more to himself than to her.

The words slid between them like a thread Charlotte didn't quite dare pull.

For a moment, she thought he might say something more — about the gondola, about that night — but he only reached for his coffee again, the moment slipping away as neatly as a closing door.

Charlotte let the silence stretch a second longer, then, lightly, she ventured:

"You know," she said, stirring her latte with a slow, absent motion, "the Met's opening a new exhibition for Valentine's Day. *Caspar David Friedrich: The Soul of Nature.*"

Jamie's glance sharpened, just slightly.

"He's considered to be one of the great German Romantic landscape painters," Charlotte added, keeping her tone casual. "Misty forests, ruins in fog, all very dramatic. His work was less about the scenery itself and more about what it felt like to stand there — alone with the wildness and silence of the world."

She let herself smile, just a little.

"Symbolism. Solitude. Anti-classical rebellion," she said lightly. "Basically everything you'd love."

For a heartbeat, she thought she saw a glimmer of amusement — real amusement — flash across Jamie's face.

But it passed almost as quickly as it came.

He only shook his head, slipping easily back behind the polished formality that had been his armor since the beginning.

"Work," he said simply, tapping his fingers once against his coffee cup. "Deadlines don't take holidays."

Charlotte nodded, schooling her expression into something smooth and bright.

"Of course," she said. "Same here. Cupid's got nothing on zoning board meetings."

They finished their coffee in polite silence, the unsaid things between them thicker than the frost lining the windows.

Outside, the pink hearts danced lightly in the windows behind them, stubborn against the gray.

And Charlotte realized, with a hollow sort of clarity, that sometimes you could lay every sign, light every candle, set every perfect scene…

And still, the story didn't unfold the way you wanted it to.

Sometimes, the heart was ready.

And the other person wasn't even reading the same page.

***

The Astor House had gone full Valentine's Day.

Charlotte pushed open the heavy oak doors, greeted by a rush of warmth and the faint scent of wood polish, roses, and something sweeter – like Ladurée candied almonds melting on the tongue.

Pink ribbons twined up the bannisters. Paper hearts fluttered from the chandeliers, their delicate shadows dancing across the faded silk walls. Even the massive grandfather clock in the front hall wore a discreet satin bow, pinned just above the glass.

In the Pine Room, the usual hush of mahogany and antique chintz had been brightened by a riot of pink tulips, white anemones, and tiny vases filled with candy hearts printed with syrupy messages: BE MINE, TRUE LOVE, KISS ME.

The bar had gotten into the spirit too.

Tonight's special: The First Lady cocktail – a sly nod to Jackie O, rumored to be inspired by the elegant concoctions once served at Martin's Tavern in D.C. (and borrowed from the DC League). The drink shimmered a soft, romantic pink – not quite a dark liquid, so still within the house rules – a delicate blend of gin, Cointreau, and lemon juice, shaken until frothy and topped with a single basil leaf.

Sweet but not cloying, bright but not biting – the kind of drink that could coax even the most cynical heart into a little holiday cheer.

She accepted a cut-crystal coupe with a murmured thanks. The frothy cocktail winked up at her like a secret.

Charlotte slid into one of the Queen Anne chairs around the committee table, smoothing the skirt of her blush pink Diane von Furstenberg wrap dress against her knees. The pink wasn't exactly her usual palette. But when Bunny had texted the group chat that morning – "On Wednesdays we wear pink" – Charlotte had smiled, pulled the dress from the back of her closet, and decided not to fight it.

Maybe she wasn't exactly one of them yet.

But she wasn't standing apart anymore either.

Around the room, the other women trickled in: Bunny Lancaster in a pastel tweed shift and heart-shaped earrings that somehow looked charming rather than kitschy; Cassandra Chao, all sleek understatement in a mauve turtleneck and diamond studs. And even

Avery Sinclair, who almost never deviated from her signature emerald green, had bent slightly to the season – arriving in a pale blush silk blouse and a rose-colored blazer, her high ponytail still glossy and sharp but softened, just a little, by the festive palette.

Avery rapped a manicured hand lightly against the table, calling the meeting to order.

"Ladies," she said, her voice smooth and unhurried, "we're finalizing details for the Galentine's party later this month."

A ripple of excitement passed through the room.

"Heart-shaped cookies are ordered. The band is confirmed. And Bunny – " she nodded graciously – "secured those miniature champagne bottles for the party favors."

Bunny beamed, her pearl bracelet jingling.

"And Charlotte," Avery continued, her smile polished but, for once, genuinely warm, "you're handling the welcome table?"

Charlotte straightened slightly, feeling the warm, easy burn of focus settle in her chest – the same feeling she usually reserved for auction previews and gallery shows.

"I'm happy to," she said, voice clear. "And I can manage the raffle table too if you need extra hands."

For a second, Avery blinked – just the briefest flicker of surprise – before she smiled again, something lighter and more real than Charlotte was used to seeing from her.

"That would be much appreciated," Avery said, nodding. "It's good to have someone so dependable."

Charlotte smiled back—steady, certain.

She wasn't chasing approval anymore.

She was building something.

The room buzzed with easy chatter and scribbled notes. Encouraged by the warmth, Charlotte cleared her throat softly.

"I had another idea," she said. "For a fundraiser to go alongside the Galentine's party."

Avery arched a brow, curious.

Charlotte pressed on, heart thudding.

"We could nominate some of our most eligible friends – guys and girls – who are willing to be 'auctioned' for charity. All in good fun. Champagne, bidding wars, Valentine's spirit, and the proceeds could go towards the literacy fund."

For a moment, there was a beat of silence.

Then Bunny let out an audible squeal, practically bouncing in her seat.

"I know someone!" she gasped. "Charles Beauford—he plays squash at the Racquet Club and has, like, the jawline of a young Kennedy. Oh my god, he and Cassandra would be perfect!"

All eyes swung to Cassandra, whose usual cool demeanor cracked – just slightly – as a faint blush crept up her neck. She waved Bunny off with a mock-glare and an expertly manicured acrylic but didn't argue.

Avery tapped her pen thoughtfully against her notepad, studying Charlotte. It was rare to catch her off guard – but, for once, she seemed genuinely weighing the idea, not just looking for the angle.

"It's bold," Avery said slowly.

Charlotte's stomach twisted – but before she could regret speaking up, Avery's mouth curved into a faint smile.

"Bold," she repeated, "but charming. I think it could work – if handled elegantly of course."

Around the table, a murmur of agreement rippled through the group, glasses lifted in soft, spontaneous toasts.

The meeting began to wrap up, women pulling coats tighter and texting Ubers. As Charlotte gathered her things, Avery looked up again.

"Oh, and one more thing," she said, her voice almost casual. "We have a box reserved for ballet Friday night. New York City Ballet's Balanchine spectacle. You should come."

Charlotte blinked – surprised, but genuinely touched. An invitation like that wasn't handed out lightly.

"I'd love to," she said warmly.

As the women drifted towards the foyer in clusters of laughter and wool coats, Charlotte slipped her phone from her pocket to check the time.

A new message flashed across the screen.

Jamie.

Can you review the updated plans for the Breuer stairwell mock-up? Need feedback before Thursday.

Charlotte stared at it for a long moment.

The old version of herself – the one desperate to prove she could keep up, that she belonged – would have answered immediately.

Instead, Charlotte slid the phone back into her bag.

The plans could wait.

Tonight was for her.

She caught up with Cassandra and Bunny by the door, their cheeks flushed from champagne and good gossip.

Outside, the city blinked with the last gleams of pink twilight. Charlotte tucked her arm through Bunny's, laughing softly as they stepped into the cold night air.

***

Friday night unfolded soft and slow, like a velvet ribbon unspooling through the city.

Charlotte tugged her heavy camel coat tighter around her cocktail dress, the February wind curling slyly through the marble arches of Lincoln Center. The plaza sparkled under the low glow of chandeliers suspended above the open air, their crystals winking like frozen stars against the dark winter sky.

Bunny, wearing a frothy pink tulle dress and a faux fur stole, linked arms with Charlotte and Cassandra as they crossed the plaza, their heels clicking smartly over the stone.

"Valentine's – and Valentinos! – at the ballet," Bunny declared, practically glowing. "Zero expectations, maximum champagne."

Cassandra smiled – a real, small smile – and adjusted her black Celine clutch under her arm. Her hair was twisted into an elegant chignon, a pair of delicate diamond drops winking at her ears.

Charlotte had chosen a glittering pink cocktail dress for the night – silly, a little girlish, but exactly what she needed. Her pearl earrings gleamed softly against her hair, a quiet echo of all the small, lovely things she was starting to remember about herself.

Inside, the lobby was a rush of soft light and bright color. Women in satin and sequins glided across the glossy marble floors; men in dark suits and velvet dinner jackets leaned against the grand staircase.

Great urns overflowing with white orchids stood at the base of the sweeping staircases, their elegant blooms glowing in the golden light, breathing a clean, delicate freshness into the air.

The scent of orchids and old perfume hung just beneath the surface – something timeless, bittersweet.

Charlotte slipped out of her coat, smoothing her dress, and followed Bunny and Cassandra towards their box – Avery's, of course – tucked high above the stage. Red velvet seats lined the small balcony, chandeliers raining gold from the ceiling, the heavy red curtains swelling and falling like a heartbeat.

The orchestra struck the first note, and for a while, Charlotte let herself be carried by the music: the sweep of violins, the dancers moving like stitched light across the stage. It was beautiful in that way heartbreak could sometimes be beautiful – fragile, fleeting, aching and perfect all at once.

At intermission, they spilled back into the gilded lobby, the hum of conversation and the clink of champagne glasses filling the air like a waltz.

Charlotte drifted towards the marble balustrade, cradling her glass, letting the scene blur and soften.

And that's when she saw him.

Jamie.

Standing near the grand staircase, coat draped neatly over one arm, his head bent towards a frail woman wrapped in a soft gray shawl. His hand hovered lightly at her back, steadying her as he helped her move through the crowd.

Charlotte stopped where she stood, the marble floor cold through the soles of her rockstuds.

Jamie's expression – so often unreadable, so often walled off – was open now. Tender. Fiercely protective.

The kind of tenderness you didn't fake. The kind you didn't even think to hide when it was real.

Something cracked open inside her, sudden and sharp.

For a second, everything else – the chandeliers, the laughter, the glittering gowns – blurred around the edges. And she saw only him, and the woman he was guiding so carefully, so reverently.

Her chest tightened painfully, memories surging unbidden. Hospital corridors washed in sterile white. The smell of hand sanitizer and fading lilies. Her mother's hand slipping quietly from hers.

Jamie wasn't guarded because he didn't feel.

He was guarded because he felt too much.

He wasn't distant because he thought he was better. He was distant because there were some things so heavy, so sharp-edged, that they couldn't be carried any other way but close to the bone.

Charlotte blinked hard, swallowing against the sudden thickness in her throat.

Cassandra appeared at her side, linking their arms lightly.

"You okay?" she asked, her voice low and careful.

Charlotte managed a small nod.

"Yeah," she said, voice steadier than she felt. "Come on. I don't want to miss the second act."

And she meant it.

Because tonight wasn't about chasing anything – not approval, not dreams, not even him.

It was about standing still for once, and letting herself see clearly.

And what she saw wasn't arrogance.

It was survival. It was grief.

It was a heart that had been broken and rebuilt, just like hers.

And for the first time, Charlotte wondered if maybe – just maybe – they weren't standing so far apart after all.

***

The second act blurred past in a shimmering haze of tulle and moonlight.

Charlotte sat quietly in her red velvet seat, but her mind wasn't on the stage.

Not on the dancers who floated like ghosts across the boards, not on the swell of the violins rising toward the chandeliers.

Her mind was caught somewhere between past and present – between the sight of Jamie's hand, steady and gentle at his mother's back, and the memory of her own mother's hand, slipping from hers like water sieving through sandcastles.

She kept stealing glances downward, toward the box where Jamie sat – so composed, so careful, so utterly unaware that someone across the theater was seeing him clearly for the first time.

By the time the curtain fell, Charlotte felt hollowed out and strange, like a snow globe that had been shaken too hard and left to settle in new, unfamiliar patterns.

She didn't say much as they bundled into their coats and drifted back into the night.

There were other plans to keep them busy – plans she'd almost forgotten in the haze of the evening.

The Galentine's Date Auction.

***

The West Village jazz club buzzed with soft laughter and clinking glasses, the air humming with energy.

It was a different world entirely from the grand, echoing splendor of Lincoln Center – and the Astor House for that matter – lower ceilings, velvet drapes, brass sconces dripping with warm, honeyed light. A narrow stage had been set up near the piano, framed by a cascade of red roses and gold bunting.

Charlotte stood near the edge of the room, smoothing the front of her fitted black dress, a clipboard tucked under her arm. She'd volunteered to help organize tonight's festivities and she'd thrown herself into it with more enthusiasm than she'd felt in weeks.

Around her, groups of girls sipped champagne and giggled behind raised hands as the date auction unfolded.

It was, against all odds, a roaring success.

Eligible bachelors and bachelorettes – curated lovingly by Bunny and Cassandra – were parading across the stage with sheepish grins, auctioned off for charity to the highest bidder.

A weekend sailing trip.

A private museum tour.

A cooking class with a "celebrity" chef.

All in good fun, all in the name of a good cause. The room crackled with laughter, teasing bids flying fast and loud.

Charlotte clapped and cheered with the rest, smiling when Charles Beauford swaggered onto the stage in a perfectly tailored blazer, and Bunny nearly toppled over her seat trying to boost Cassandra's paddle into the air.

Cassandra, for her part, turned a shade of pink that almost matched the roses onstage but didn't lower her hand – and ended up winning him with a triumphant flourish.

Charlotte laughed with the others, feeling, for once, a little less like an outsider. A little more like she belonged.

And then, as the evening began to wind down, the final name was called.

Charlotte wasn't really listening at first, still scribbling notes on her clipboard.

But then she heard it.

Jamie Harrison.

Her head snapped up so fast she nearly knocked over her champagne flute.

And there he was – striding onto the stage in dark jeans and a navy jacket, hands tucked loosely in his pockets, a bemused smile tugging at his mouth.

The room collectively leaned forward.

Jamie was... well, Jamie.

Broad-shouldered.

Sharp-eyed.

Disastrously handsome in a way that seemed almost unfair in this setting, where most of the other bachelors had looked charmingly awkward at best.

Charlotte's heart stuttered painfully.

She told herself she wouldn't bid. That it would be too obvious. Too foolish. Too unprofessional.

But before she could even think about it, before anyone else could lift a paddle – Avery's hand shot into the air.

"Five hundred!" she called out, her voice bright and clear.

The room went silent for a beat, stunned by the boldness.

The auctioneer blinked, then grinned. "Any other bids?"

No one moved. Not fast enough.

"Going once," he said, laughing. "Going twice."

Charlotte's breath caught somewhere between her ribs.

"Sold!"

Avery stood up to accept her prize, all grace and polished charm, her champagne flute glinting under the lights.

Charlotte felt something sharp and ugly twist low in her stomach.

It wasn't just the winning bid.

It was the way Avery smiled afterward – all bright triumph and barely concealed satisfaction. The way Jamie dipped his head politely toward her, not quite smiling back.

Charlotte didn't wait to see more.

She slipped her clipboard onto a nearby table, grabbed her coat, and made her way through the crowd, the cold night rushing up to meet her as she pushed open the door.

The sidewalk glittered under the streetlamps, brittle and sharp.

Charlotte stood for a moment, wrapping her coat tighter, letting the city blur and whirl around her – she was spinning from the shock of it all.

She had wanted so badly to believe that maybe – just maybe – there was something real between her and Jamie weren't standing so far apart after all.

But tonight, the distance felt wider than ever.

A distance that may be too far for her to cross.

Chapter 7: March – City Advocacy Day

March was the month when New Yorkers dared to hope again. The flower beds along Madison Avenue had begun to sprout tulips and daffodils, their green shoots pushing stubbornly through the iron-colored soil like tiny, defiant promises that winter was finally loosening its grip.

Storefront windows blinked with new spring displays – pastel dresses, polished loafers, artfully arranged picnic baskets – while salt-streaked sidewalks and the lingering bite in the air reminded everyone not to trust the season just yet. Taxi cabs splashed through puddles left by melting snowbanks, and the scent of wet concrete and brewing coffee curled up through sidewalk grates.

Somewhere, faint but steady, the city thrummed with the first, fragile heartbeat of spring.

The morning of City Advocacy Day dawned gray and soft, the kind of March day that hinted – falsely – at warmth to come.

City Advocacy Day was a Junior League tradition and a requirement for all provisional members hoping to join full-time at the end of the first year of service. Each woman was expected to choose a cause that she cared about, stand at the podium at City Hall, and make her voice heard. It was about civic engagement, yes, but also about courage, clarity, and learning how to speak not just for oneself, but for others.

Charlotte stood in front of her full-length mirror, tugging at the hem of her soft gray Carolina Herrera skirt set – a vintage two-piece that had once belonged to her mother.

The fabric was delicate but strong, a whisper of structure and elegance that made her feel somehow steadier just wearing it. The pencil skirt hit just below her knee, the matching jacket nipped in smartly at the waist and pearl buttons winked subtly in the pale morning light.

She tried to ignore the tight coil of nerves gathering in her stomach.

"Stop fidgeting," Ivy said from her perch on the windowsill, sipping black coffee from a chipped mug that read Well-Behaved Women Rarely Make History.

She was still in faded flannel pajama pants and a Harvard sweatshirt, looking maddeningly serene.

"I'm going to jumble every sentence like it's a Scrabble board," Charlotte muttered, smoothing the jacket for the fourth time.

"You look like someone City Hall's going to take seriously," Ivy said, crossing the room. "Even if your verbs get tangled. Worst case, you triple-word-score your way through it."

She set her mug down and crossed the room, plucking an invisible piece of lint from Charlotte's shoulder with a practiced flick.

"Remember – you're not asking for a favor. You're making the case for something that matters."

Clementine let out an affirmatory whoof. Charlotte exhaled slowly, nodding.

Arts funding.

Access for women and girls.

The very things that had made her who she was — Saturday morning museum trips, school plays, sketchbooks tucked under her arm like a second heartbeat. Small moments that had quietly built the dream that one day, she might live and work among the arts, not just admire them from afar. Proof that the arts mattered — not as luxuries, but as lifelines.

"I still feel ridiculous," Charlotte admitted, trying to laugh it off.

"Good," Ivy said. "If you're not at least a little scared, you're not aiming high enough."

It was the kind of thing Ivy could say without sounding glib.

After all, she'd studied political science, protested everything from climate change to rent hikes, and once gotten herself politely escorted out of a city council meeting for refusing to relinquish the mic. Advocacy ran in her blood.

Charlotte pinned her Junior League nametag to her lapel, the gold script gleaming against the soft dove-gray wool.

"So," Ivy said casually, leaning against the doorframe as Charlotte gathered her things, "are we just pretending the date auction night never happened?"

Charlotte froze for half a heartbeat — just long enough for Ivy to notice — and then shrugged, slipping her portfolio into her tote bag with a little more force than necessary.

"Nothing to pretend," she said lightly. "Avery bought a date. Jamie smiled and said thank you. Life moves on."

Ivy gave her a long, assessing look but, mercifully, didn't push.

Charlotte threw on her trench coat, buttoned it neatly to her throat, and lifted her chin.

She was done chasing anyone who didn't choose her. Done hoping the story might bend toward a fairytale ending if she just wished hard enough.

Today wasn't about Jamie.

Today was about standing up, speaking out, and being seen – for herself.

"Wish me luck," Charlotte said, offering a wobbly but determined smile.

"You don't need it," Ivy said, tossing her a wink. "Go knock 'em dead, Hastings."

Charlotte pulled open the door and stepped into the crisp morning air, the first faint cracks of sunlight breaking through the cloud cover above Madison Avenue.

The street stretched wide and shimmering before her, lined with hopeful blooms and shop windows full of promises.

***

City Hall rose pale and proud at the edge of City Hall Park, its marble facade catching the first watery gleam of morning sun. Around it, the bare trees stretched their spindly branches towards the misty March sky, tiny green buds just beginning to bristle with the first daring hints of spring.

Originally constructed in the early 1800's, the building stood like a quiet testament to New York's resilience. Part French Renaissance, part American Georgian, all stubborn beauty. It had survived yellow fever, labor strikes, fires, and fashion trends, its marble steps worn smooth by two centuries of hope and heartbreak. The soaring rotunda inside – framed by fluted Corinthian columns and a domed ceiling – had cradled presidents, poets, and protestors alike.

Charlotte gathered with her fellow League members just outside the gates of City Hall Park, a pastel blur of powder blue, lilac, blush pink, and butter yellow. They looked, she thought wryly, like a box of Ladurée macarons that had tipped over on the cobblestones.

Bunny Lancaster adjusted the bow of her silk blouse, glancing around nervously.

"Anyone else feel like they're about to take the SATs?" she stage-whispered.

Charlotte clutched her tote tighter, feeling the comforting weight of her portfolio inside. Around them, the city stirred – the soft thrum of subway grates, the snap of a newspaper folding under a vendor's hand, the sharp scent of coffee and wet pavement rising like steam.

Inside, the building was quieter, almost holy.

Marble floors gleamed under the worn tread of history. At the center, the rotunda opened skyward, white stone columns lifting the heavy dome as if they had all the time in the world.

Beneath their feet, the ghosts of a thousand declarations, oaths, and whispered hopes seemed to hum.

Charlotte's pearl earrings winked at her ears, steady, quiet things, like beacons.

The chamber doors opened.

Charlotte swallowed hard, feeling the nerves ricochet against her ribs.

It was her turn to speak.

"You've got this," Ivy's voice echoed from memory. "You make arts funding sound glamorous."

***

Charlotte crossed the marble floor towards the podium, her sensible heels clicking softly in the cavernous space. A hush fell over the room, a scattering of councilmembers, staffers, and League members in pastel suits lined up neatly in the gallery.

She set her notes on the podium, hands steady.

And she began.

"Good morning. My name is Charlotte Hastings, and I'm here today on behalf of the New York Junior League to advocate for increased funding and access to arts education for women and girls across our city."

Her voice was clear – not booming, not trembling – just steady enough to carry across the rotunda.

"I stand here because of a public arts program," Charlotte continued. "Because a teacher handed me a sketchbook in second grade and said, 'Go draw your dreams.' Because a city-funded museum let me wander for hours on Saturdays, believing that art belonged to me – not just to the people whose names were carved into the marble."

She let that hang for half a heartbeat.

Around her, faces softened. Pens stilled.

"Study after study shows that access to the arts improves academic outcomes, fosters confidence, builds critical thinking. Girls who engage with the arts are more likely to graduate, to pursue higher education, to step into leadership roles. They learn to tell their own stories – and to listen to the stories of others."

She smiled, letting a touch of warmth color her voice.

"In a city that prides itself on being the creative capital of the world, we have a responsibility to ensure that creativity isn't a privilege. It's a right."

She finished with a simple plea.

"Fund the future. Fund the voices waiting to be heard."

A beat of silence.

And then – applause. Real applause, warm and sustained.

Charlotte stepped back from the podium, cheeks flushed and heart pounding, blinking against the sudden brightness of the marble room.

And that's when she saw him.

Jamie Harrison, leaning casually against a marble column in the back, arms folded loosely across his chest, watching her.

And smiling – a small, unguarded smile that she felt all the way to her toes.

But he wasn't the only familiar face.

Near the center aisle, impeccably dressed in a navy tweed coat and a strand of pearls that seemed to glow in the light, sat Barbara Fairchild.

Charlotte's breath caught.

Barbara was smiling, too – not the polite, encouraging smile given to any young woman making her first civic speech. This was smaller, sharper, and infinitely prouder, as if she'd expected nothing less and was merely pleased to see the rest of the world catching up.

Charlotte gave the faintest tilt of her head – not quite a nod, just enough of a silent thank-you.

Barbara responded with a small, regal dip of her chin, the kind that carried the weight of generations behind it.

The councilwoman in a sunflower-yellow blazer approached next, her heels clicking smartly across the marble.

"You made a fine case, Miss Hastings," she said, pressing a business card into Charlotte's hand with a knowing smile. "Don't be surprised if you see your name in tomorrow's Times. We need more voices like yours."

Charlotte stammered out a thank-you, clutching the card like it was spun gold.

The applause faded, replaced by the low murmur of the next speaker taking the podium. But Charlotte hardly heard it. She gathered her notes carefully, tucking them into her tote.

As she turned to leave, Barbara Fairchild swept past – no words, just the faintest brush of her gloved hand against Charlotte's elbow, a touch so fleeting it felt almost imagined.

Outside, the city roared back to life – taxis honking, pigeons scattering across City Hall Park, tulip buds trembling in the cold March breeze.

Charlotte stood on the marble steps for a long moment, letting it sink in.

It wasn't just a speech.

It wasn't just a moment.

It was the beginning of something bigger – something she had built with her own voice.

And maybe, just maybe, it was only the beginning.

***

Word moves fast when you're in The New York Times.

Fast enough, apparently, to land you a coveted spot on Avery Sinclair's tightly guarded tennis calendar by Monday afternoon.

The Sinclair Club wasn't the kind of place you joined — it was the kind of place you were born into.

Memberships passed down like heirlooms, locker keys engraved with names that had graced the social register for generations. Court times weren't booked, they were inherited.

Charlotte practically bounced on the balls of her feet as she waited near the entrance to Court Three, her racquet tucked under one arm.

The courts were indoors — smooth, polished clay glowing under a web of skylights, with the late March sun dancing across the rafters. The air smelled gloriously of fresh tennis balls and clean resin, the faint tang of exertion humming just under the bright, open space.

She loved tennis.

Always had.

Still, as she adjusted the grip on her racquet, a flicker of suspicion lingered just beneath her excitement.

After the date auction fiasco, after watching Avery raise that paddle without hesitation, it wasn't lost on Charlotte that there might be more to today's invitation than just a casual hit-around.

But for once, she wasn't going to second-guess every good thing that came her way.

Sometimes you had to trust that people showed up for you, even if it looked different than you expected.

Avery appeared from the far end of the court, all crisp whites and calm authority. Her skirt swayed neatly with each stride, her high ponytail gleaming under the skylights, her sneakers pristine.

They rallied easily at first – warm-up volleys that sharpened into something faster, lighter, more competitive. Charlotte moved instinctively, her body remembering the rhythm of it, the quick footwork, the satisfying pop of the ball meeting the sweet spot of the strings.

After a few brisk points, Avery called a break and jogged towards the bench, tossing Charlotte a chilled bottle of water.

"You surprised me at City Advocacy Day," Avery said, casual as a passing serve.

"You mean... the speech?" Charlotte caught the bottle with a practiced flick of her wrist.

Avery nodded once, her approval quiet but unmistakable.

"You didn't just speak. You commanded the room."

Charlotte flushed slightly, but she held Avery's gaze this time.

Avery wiped a hand lightly across her forehead and sat back against the bench.

"Our mothers were best friends," she said, the words almost startling in their directness. "Before either of us could spell Junior League."

Charlotte blinked. She hadn't known.

"They built this city's art scene in pearls and kitten heels," Avery said, a rare fondness flickering across her polished exterior. "When your mother got sick, she asked mine for one last favor."

She paused, letting the weight of it settle.

"She asked her to make sure you made it here. Not just into the League. Into the world."

Charlotte swallowed hard, the floor under her sneakers suddenly feeling very solid, very real.

"I've been tough on you," Avery said, smiling just slightly. "But sometimes, all you really need in life is league, love, and a little lipstick."

The words slipped out so easily, but they landed with a quiet kind of grace. Like a bridge being built between two hearts – one step at a time.

Charlotte laughed, a real laugh, fresh and full and free. The kind that cracked something old and afraid wide open.

Avery rose, smoothing the front of her skirt.

"I arranged something for you," she said lightly. "It's upstairs."

Still a little breathless from tennis and revelation alike, Charlotte followed her through the winding halls of the club – past framed black-and-white photographs of legendary matches and glinting silver trophy cases.

The dining room was near-empty at this hour, late afternoon sunlight streaming in broad, golden bands across the hardwood floors.

And at a small table tucked in the far corner – jacket draped over the back of his chair, hair slightly mussed – sat Jamie Harrison.

He rose immediately at the sight of her, straightening his cuffs and smiling in that quiet, devastating way that seemed to cut straight through her.

Charlotte stood still for half a heartbeat.

And then the pieces fit together.

Avery hadn't bought Jamie's date at the auction for herself. She had bought it for Charlotte.

The realization filled her with a soft, fierce heat – something closer to gratitude than she could name.

Across the room, Avery caught her eye and gave the faintest nod – barely more than a shift of her chin – but it said everything:

You're not alone. You never were.

Charlotte crossed the room slowly, her tennis skirt brushing against her legs, her racquet tucked under one arm like a promise.

Jamie pulled out her chair with a quiet, instinctive grace.

"You stopped the whole room at city hall," he said simply, once she was seated. "You stopped me."

Charlotte smiled back – steady, luminous, unafraid.

Outside, the March light gleamed against the city's spires, promising spring.

Inside, Charlotte realized she was no longer standing at the edge of things.

She was already home.

Chapter 8: April – Savor the Spring

The ferry cut cleanly through the slate-gray water, whitecaps slapping against the hull as the island crept into view – weathered shingles, windswept dunes, and the faintest flicker of yellow along the horizon, like a promise half-whispered – the daffodils were waiting.

Charlotte leaned on the railing, hair wind-whipped, cheeks flushed pink from the cold.

Clementine, wrapped in a lemon-yellow Barbour coat, sprawled between her and Ivy, uninterested in the conversation but deeply invested in her nap.

"I swear, if Daffodil Weekend didn't exist, we'd have had to invent it," Ivy said, tucking her hair into her collar. "It's the only thing that makes March worth surviving."

Charlotte smiled. "It feels like a memory before we even get there."

They had been coming to Nantucket for the festival since before they could walk – Charlotte in smocked dresses and Ivy in lopsided daisy crowns, their mothers pulling them through town in tiny red Radio Flyer wagons decked out in fresh blooms. Daffodils in their hair, juice boxes in hand, waving to the vintage car parade like they were royalty. It was a tradition built into their bones.

The air smelled of salt and cold iron, that bracing scent that only came thirty miles out at sea. Sunlight played across the water like a slow-motion shimmer, dancing off whitecaps in a way that made everything feel just a little bit enchanted – like the ferry wasn't taking them to an island but to another version of their lives.

"So." Ivy slanted a sideways glance. "Tell me everything. The Jamie situation."

Charlotte didn't rush the smile. "It started with a tennis match."

Ivy blinked. "I'm sorry, what?"

"Avery invited me to the Sinclair Club," Charlotte said. "Said she had a free court and wanted to talk about Advocacy Day. We played. And then, afterwards, she handed me a bottle of water, told me I might want to fix my hair, and said someone was waiting upstairs."

Ivy's eyes narrowed, gears turning. "She didn't."

"She did."

"Was he—"

Charlotte nodded. "Jamie. Sitting in the far corner of the dining room, jacket over the back of his chair, flipping through The New Yorker. Like it was the most ordinary thing in the world."

Ivy stared at her. "She gave you his auction date."

"She never said it out loud," Charlotte said. "She didn't have to."

There was a pause as the truth settled between them.

"And?" Ivy prompted. "How was it?"

Charlotte turned back towards the horizon, watching the island rise slowly from the sea. "It was quiet. Simple. No pressure. No pretense."

She let the words find her slowly, like they had to be earned. "He made me feel like… nothing about me needed adjusting. Like I wasn't performing or proving or being weighed."

Ivy was quiet for a moment.

"And that surprised you?"

Charlotte nodded once. "It surprised me how much I wanted to stay in that moment."

They stood there in silence, the ferry humming beneath them, salt air curling through their hair.

"I think Avery was keeping a promise," Charlotte said softly.

"To your mom?"

"To both of us."

Ivy smiled. "High praise."

"Don't make me regret it."

***

They wandered slowly down Main Street, Clementine trotting proudly ahead like she was inspecting the daffodil garlands herself. People stopped every few feet to greet her – shopkeepers, tourists, a toddler gripping a pinwheel – bending down to scratch behind her ears and murmur their respects like she was the town's unofficial mayor.

"She knows," Ivy said solemnly, as a silver-haired woman in a lemon sweater cooed, "Good to see you again, Miss Clementine."

"Knows what?" Charlotte asked, amused.

"That she runs this island. That we're just the supporting cast."

Clementine glanced back at them with the calm superiority of someone who'd long accepted her legacy status.

Nantucket had outdone itself this year. Every window box and stoop seemed to be bursting with blossoms – tulips, daffodils, buttercup-yellow ranunculus cascading like laughter over white-painted fences. A jazz trio played softly outside the Chamber of Commerce, their instruments gleaming in the sun. Somewhere, someone was handing out lemon scones from a wicker basket tied with a yellow bow.

Charlotte breathed it all in – the scent of early lilac, the clang of bike bells, the rustle of linen skirts and dog leashes and old memories she didn't know she still carried.

"So," Ivy said, skipping ahead half a step, "tell me about this floral fever dream you're co-chairing."

"Savor the Spring," Charlotte said, her voice warming just from saying it. "It's the final League gala of the season. We're hosting it at the Breuer."

Ivy turned. "Our Breuer?"

Charlotte nodded. "Sotheby's is finally opening up the west gallery. Jamie's been overseeing the restoration for months. He offered to let us use it early."

Ivy blinked. "From scaffolding and latte runs to a black-tie fundraiser. That's a glow-up."

Charlotte smiled. "We've been working together on it since the fall. He knows every stone in that building. I know every light fixture. Now we just have to fill it with roses and get everyone in heels."

"You thrive in chaos. You just prefer it with a guest list."

They passed a boutique with pale blue shutters and a daffodil-lined entryway. In the window, a yellow gown glowed like it had been lit from within – pleated chiffon, a delicate keyhole back, and a thin satin belt tied like a whisper around the waist.

Charlotte stopped.

"That's it," Ivy said immediately.

Charlotte tilted her head. "Too... much?"

"It's spring. You're co-hosting. You've survived drama, heartbreak, construction dust, and one very powerful woman's silent approval. Buy the dress."

Charlotte hesitated, and Ivy gently bumped her shoulder.

"Look," she said, quieter now, "you don't have to protect yourself from joy. Not everything beautiful is waiting to disappoint you."

Charlotte looked at the gown again, at the flicker of herself reflected in the shop glass – windblown, a little sun-kissed, steadier than she used to be.

Then, with a soft smile, she said, "You should come."

Ivy arched an eyebrow. "To the gala?"

"Why not?" Charlotte said. "You've been helping me behind the scenes all year. Even if no one else saw it, I did."

Ivy's expression shifted, the humor dropping into something warmer. "That's what best friends do, Hastings. We show up. Even when it's not our name on the invite."

Charlotte smiled. "So? Will you?"

"I'll wear black," Ivy deadpanned. "Blend in with the waitstaff."

Charlotte laughed. "Bring whoever you want. Seriously."

Ivy looked at her for a long moment, then nodded. "I'll bring the girl I've been seeing. If that's cool."

Charlotte's smile turned into something real, something rooted. "It's very cool."

And just like that, she opened the door to the boutique, and the bell chimed like a beginning.

***

The Breuer smelled like sawdust, roses, and last-minute miracles.

It was nearly midnight, and the main gallery was a soft blur of upturned chairs, half-unpacked crates, and wilting takeout containers. Charlotte stood barefoot in the center of it all, her heels abandoned somewhere by the freight elevator, her hair twisted into a pencil-stabbed knot.

She adjusted a table setting for the fourth time, then stepped back and squinted.

"It's crooked," Jamie's voice called from behind her. "But only if you're standing just so and deeply type-A."

Charlotte turned to find him leaning against a ladder, sleeves rolled up, a carpenter's pencil tucked behind one ear. He looked maddeningly composed for someone who had just spent the last hour hoisting planters the size of bathtubs up two flights of stone stairs.

"I don't need your sarcasm right now," she said.

"I wasn't being sarcastic." His tone was even. Mild. "I'm impressed."

He walked towards her slowly, hands tucked into the pockets of his work pants. The kind of unhurried pace that said he had nothing to prove – and no desire to perform.

"You've turned a raw concrete gallery into something that smells like a French meadow and feels like a storybook."

She narrowed her eyes. "You missed your calling as a poet."

Jamie tilted his head. "I'm not trying to impress anyone."

That was the maddening thing about him – he meant it. He never played the room. He just was – deliberate, understated, observant in a way that made her feel exposed and seen at the same time.

They stood in silence for a moment, the kind that stretched without strain. Outside, the city throbbed in muted pulses – headlights drifting past, a siren low and distant.

Charlotte exhaled. "Something's missing."

He lifted an eyebrow. "Your shoes? Sanity?"

She almost smiled, but it slipped. "The light fixture. The glass bloom installation for the stairwell. It should've arrived today."

Jamie's expression didn't change. He absorbed the information like stone absorbs rain – without flinch, without fuss.

"Then I'll find it."

"You're being too calm," she said, narrowing her eyes. "That means it's bad."

"I don't know that it's bad," he said quietly. "And either way, calm is useful. I'll track it down."

"Jamie—"

He stepped closer, but not too close. Just enough that she had to tilt her chin slightly to meet his eyes.

He smelled like fresh soap and clean sweat – no cologne, no charm offensive, just an unstudied kind of cleanliness that made her pulse stumble. It was maddening, how he always smelled like honesty. Like effort. Like he'd scrubbed paint off his hands ten minutes ago and never thought twice about the impression he left behind.

It was the kind of scent that didn't ask to be noticed – which only made it harder to ignore.

"I said I'll take care of it."

Charlotte held his gaze. He didn't look smug. He didn't smile. There was no performance, no invitation, no attempt to win her over.

Just quiet certainty.

It shook her more than flowers ever could.

"I hate asking for help," she admitted, her voice low now. Steadier than she felt.

"I know," he said. "That's why I didn't wait for you to ask."

She could have said something. About the lighting. About the linens. About anything.

But instead she stood still, rooted in the weight of his words, the impossible steadiness of him, the quiet hum of wanting something she hadn't planned for.

He watched her for a beat longer, then nodded once – formal, almost courtly – and turned away.

"You're going to be the reason this night works," he said, over his shoulder.

And then he was gone. No dramatic exit, no lingering look. Just the soft sound of his Chelsea boots down the corridor, and the scent of spring and sweat and something unspoken hanging in the air behind him.

***

By six o'clock, the Breuer had bloomed.

Gone were the tarps and toolboxes. In their place – towering floral columns, white orchards, trailing wisteria, glass orbs filled with floating votives, and the gentle murmur of a string quartet tuning up in the corner.

Charlotte stood near the gallery entrance, her headset gently tucked behind her ear. Her yellow gown moved with her like liquid silk, a quiet triumph of chiffon and soft strength. Yellow hadn't typically been her color of choice, but today it felt right – like sunshine.

She'd stopped checking her clipboard twenty minutes ago. The place was ready. She was ready.

And just as promised – the missing light fixture was suspended above the west stairwell, a glowing canopy of blown-glass blossoms that caught the overhead light like dew.

She hadn't asked. She didn't need to. Jamie had handled it.

Of course he had.

***

The main floor thrummed with warm chatter and clinking glasses. At the flower crown station, Ivy had somehow convinced a city councilwoman to wear a chamomile tiara.

Nearby, a pastel-skirted artist sketched guests as they laughed and posed in floral-print gowns and crinkled linen suits, her hand moving in fluid strokes as portraits were slipped into vellum envelopes tied with pale green twine.

Charlotte moved through the room with unhurried grace, exchanging hugs, air kisses, and quiet thank-you's.

As she passed the champagne bar, someone murmured with a soft smile, "this doesn't feel like a fundraiser. It feels like a love letter to spring."

She felt it too – in the shimmer of the lighting, in the sound of Ivy's easy laughter from across the room, in the bouquet of confidence blooming quietly in her chest.

At one point, she felt him before she saw him.

Jamie didn't make an entrance. He just appeared – near the back wall, half-shadowed besides a tall floral installation, hands in his pockets, eyes already on her.

No suit jacket. No fanfare.

Just a quiet presence that settled something in her.

They didn't speak. Not yet. But she nodded once, and he nodded back. It was enough.

***

Just before nine, a soft chime rang out from the speakers.

Avery stepped onto the small stage at the front of the gallery, dressed in a deep emerald gown that gleamed like glass under the uplights. The room stilled on cue – the subtle but unmistakable hush of people who had learned to listen when she spoke.

"As many of you know," she began, "Savor the Spring is one of the League's most cherished traditions – a celebration of community, service, and the women who make this city bloom in more ways than one."

Her voice was calm, polished – but when she glanced across the crowd and her gaze caught Charlotte's, something flickered. Not nerves. Something quieter. Older.

"This year," Avery continued, "we were lucky to have a co-chair who brought not only vision and elegance, but extraordinary resilience. Someone who wrangled florists, soothed donors, chased down a missing art installation—" she paused, and a ripple of laughter passed through the room— "and somehow still managed to make it all look effortless."

"But more than that," she said, and her voice softened, "she showed us what it means to lead with both conviction and grace. To advocate for the arts, for equity, for the value of women's voices in every corner of this city."

Avery paused again, but this time it wasn't for effect.

"It is my great honor to announce a new recognition tonight – one we hope to give for many years to come. The Eleanor Hastings Provisional Excellence Award."

There was a beat of silence. Then a collective inhale – and applause.

"She was one of us," Avery went on, her voice quieter now. "A League member, yes. But also an artist, a mother, and a believer in small, consistent acts of beauty. The kind that don't always make headlines – but change lives anyway."

"And like her," Avery said, turning toward Charlotte now, "her daughter has made this League better. This city better. This night – unforgettable."

The applause swelled again, louder now. The kind that reached your ribs.

Charlotte blinked, stunned, and let the sound wrap around her.

A woman from the committee stepped forward with a small gold pin – a white orchid, cast in soft shine. It was fastened to the neckline of Charlotte's gown with delicate precision, though her hands shook slightly when she touched it.

Avery leaned in. Not for the crowd. Just for her.

"She'd be so proud of you," she said, quiet and certain.

Charlotte didn't cry. She didn't have to. The moment held her – a blend of legacy and arrival, of loss and recognition, of something finally, quietly, becoming whole.

As she stepped off the stage, someone handed her a champagne flute. Someone else touched her arm and said, "She'd be proud."

***

After the award, the night unfolded in golden waves.

There was dancing – the kind that started politely and spiraled into barefoot spins and champagne-fueled twirls. Ivy pulled Charlotte into a loop around the room to Dancing in the Moonlight, only to hand her off to a donor in pink sequins with surprisingly good rhythm. Someone started a conga line. Someone else sabered a bottle of rosé on the terrace.

Laughter spilled through the Breuer like sunlight through stained glass. Elder League members toasted with younger ones. A Junior League husband DJ'd an impromptu remix of Crazy in Love and Clair de Lune, and somehow – it worked.

People hugged longer than they meant to. They stayed later than they planned. They didn't want to leave.

Charlotte didn't either.

She wore the yellow gown like it had always belonged to her. She laughed until her stomach hurt. She forgot to check her headset. She forgot to worry. When Jamie caught her eye from across the room, she didn't look away.

It was joy, unguarded. And it lasted.

***

The Breuer was quiet again.

The quartet had packed up. The last glass had been collected. Guests had vanished into the warm City night.

Now only petals and confetti remained – curled like secrets across the stone floors.

Charlotte stood in the center of it all, barefoot, the hem of her gown dusted with pollen and glitter. Her orchid pin still gleamed at her shoulder.

Jamie was across the room folding chairs, sleeves rolled, bow-tie hanging daftly, undone, at either side of his neck. For once, he looked almost… peaceful.

They hadn't said much in the business of the night. But the silence wasn't awkward, it was easy. Familiar. Like the space between verses in a song that they already knew by heart.

Jamie crossed the room with a stack of linens, pausing beside her like it was the most natural thing in the world.

"You still standing?" he asked.

"Barely," she said, smiling. "But it's the good kind of tired."

He nodded. "You pulled it off."

She looked around – the trailing florals, the glowing light fixture, the empty champagne towers. The warmth still clinging to the walls like a benediction.

We pulled it off, she thought. But she didn't say it.

She stepped towards him, close enough to smooth the line of his shirt cuff.

"I think I'm finally a New Yorker," she murmured, mostly to herself.

And then – with no pretense, no performance, just a deep, quiet certainty – he looked deep into her eyes.

"Kiss me."

The moment his mouth found hers, the rest of the world seemed to hush – the buzz of the City below, the faint rattle of glassware in the distance, even the lingering chatter in her own head. It all went still.

His hand cupped her jaw with surprising gentleness, his thumb grazing the hinge of her cheek like he'd been waiting all night to memorize the shape of her face. Her hands found his shirt – still warm, still smelling faintly of clean linen and work – and clung there, needing something to hold onto as her knees gave just slightly beneath her.

It wasn't slow. It wasn't tentative. It was the kind of kiss that spilled over months of near-misses, of sidelong glances and unspoken what-ifs. It was gravity and spark and every hour they'd spent in the Breuer pretending not to want more.

And she felt it everywhere – in her fingertips, in the center of her chest where something soft and aching had been waiting for a sign that it was safe to bloom.

When they pulled apart, she stayed close – breath shallow, heart skittering like a hummingbird.

Jamie looked at her like he didn't quite trust himself to speak.

"Worth the wait?" he asked softly.

Charlotte was still catching her breath, but her smile – slow, radiant, undeniable – said everything.

"More," she said. "So much more."

***

The mimosa pitcher was already half-empty by the time Charlotte arrived — which, judging by the sparkle in Bunny's earrings and the trail of citrus peels across the table, meant she was precisely on time.

"Here she is!" Cassandra crowed, waving her over with a linen napkin. "Our golden girl!"

Charlotte slid into the last open seat on the sunny patio at Café Cluny, flushed from the walk and still glowing from the night before. Ivy passed her a champagne flute with an approving smile and a dramatic tilt of her sunglasses.

"You missed the toast," Ivy said. "But don't worry — I made it about myself."

"You always do," Charlotte replied, grinning.

The table was a riot of lemon-yellow tulips, half-eaten pastries, and handbags wedged between champagne buckets. Everyone was still wearing some trace of last night's gala — a daisy crown, a floral scrunchie, glitter smudged across a cheekbone. It felt less like the aftermath of a formal event and more like the morning after a secret club initiation.

Except this time, Charlotte wasn't watching from the edge.

She was part of it.

Across the table, Avery sat in a crisp white shirtdress, her sunglasses tucked into her collar, sipping coffee like it was a controlled art. When Charlotte caught her eye, Avery gave the faintest nod — not perfunctory, not polite. Real.

And Charlotte nodded back.

Her phone buzzed gently in her lap. She glanced down at the screen.

Jamie: *7 p.m. at The Guggenheim. I plan to get lost in the art—and in you.*

She smiled, tucking the phone face-down beside her plate.

Bunny launched into a dramatic reenactment of someone's failed silent auction bid. Ivy was swirling her mimosa like it was an art form. The sun caught the edge of Charlotte's orchid pin – still fastened to the neckline of her wrap dress – and it gleamed like something ancient and permanent.

For the first time since moving to New York, Charlotte didn't feel like she was catching up.

She felt like she belonged.

Afterword

The Junior League has played a meaningful role in my life, and I hope that this story gave you a glimpse into why. What began as a way to get involved in my city and meet new friends quickly became something more – a source of strength, purpose, community, and joy.

The League has introduced me to extraordinary women, helped me connect with my city in new ways, and reminded me what's possible when we show up for each other — consistently, imperfectly, and with heart.

If Charlotte's journey resonated with you and you're curious about finding your own chapter of the League, I encourage you to explore the work being done across the globe.

To find a Junior League chapter near you or learn more about the organization, visit: https://thejuniorleagueinternational.org

To support the League's mission of empowering women and transforming communities, you can also donate directly through the site.

Whether you join, support, or simply cheer from the sidelines — thank you for being part of this story.

We're all better when we lift each other up.

With love and gratitude,

M. Gorman

Made in United States
North Haven, CT
24 April 2025